Mariah Marcelo:

More Than I Ever Wanted

Deszané Flowers

ISBN: 9780578294391

First printing edition 2023

Cover illustrated by Sunsearay Jacobus

Table of Contents

Dedication and Thanks

To those who believed in my many talents.
To my mom for always encouraging me to reach beyond my goals.
To my grandmother for her endless love and support.
To my husband for the inspiration.
To my family, who supports me no matter what.
To the girl who thinks she can't. Baby girl, you can.

Chapter 1:

The Start

I woke up before my alarm, feeling anxious. It was the first day of my new job. This is different from law school or my internship. No more guidance, it was all real now. From my internship, I scored a job at Parkers and Parkers Law Firm doing some paralegal work, while I waited for my bar exam results. If you're lucky, the internship you have can turn into a job after law school. Once I passed the bar exam, I would be among that bunch.

To avoid being late on my first day or maybe I was just anxious, I picked my clothes out the night before. I decided to dress for the spring weather, a black business skirt suit would do the trick. A black pencil skirt with a matching black blazer, a pink button-down shirt, and the new nude red bottoms that were gifted to me as a graduation gift. You know what they say, "Look the part". Feeling confident is the next best thing to being it, right? I grabbed my tea, gave one last glance, and headed out the door.

As soon as I stepped off of the elevator the brisk temperature was the first thing to greet me. I dressed for the weather outside, but maybe a skirt wasn't the best choice. As I stood and waited on the lead paralegal as I was directed to do by the receptionist, I observed the room. Everyone seemed so welcoming, a few people greeted me as we walked through the office, but that did not ease the way I was feeling.

"Good morning Mariah", the lead paralegal said as she walked to me with her hand out waiting for me to shake it. I was always weary of shaking hands, but that didn't stop the automatic impulse I had to do it anyways. "I am Bernie, the lead paralegal here. Mr. Parker has told me so much about you. We're all excited to have you on our team." I finish the hand shake and reply, "Good morning, and thank you. I'm excited to be here as well!" Thinking I hope she didn't realize my hand was shaking from nerves.

She ushered me into a small conference room, there's two small desks, each with a computer and office supplies. The room is as cold as the lobby. "Here is where you will be for today. Don't get too comfortable. IT hasn't finished setting up your computer in your office. I'll be back shortly with some cases for you to work on. If you have any questions, just let me know!" I nodded, grinned, and set my things down on the desk. Even though I have worked here before, this time felt new.

The first day at the office was intimidating to say the least. In law school, they teach the basis of law and the theory of how the law should be interpreted. But no one teaches you how to be a lawyer. Before I was under the guidance of lead partner Bill Parkers, now I am on my own. I said a prayer, took a deep breath, and gave myself some reaffirming words. The paralegal returned and it was time to put this knowledge to work. Until I passed the bar, they would offer me the cases that weren't assigned to anyone until I started getting my own clientele. I was just excited to be there and would take whatever I could get.

I knew that I wanted to become a lawyer and knew I wanted to finish law school. The entire process tested my dedication, from applying to finishing school to now passing the bar. From the start I promised myself that I would finish, no matter what and I did just that. All of this left me no time for extracurricular activities, which included dating. Not that I wasn't interested; I just couldn't see how I'd have the time for a boyfriend.

Now, having school out of the way and on to starting my career, I can go back and focus on some of the things I enjoy doing. I guess I can attempt to date now that I am relieved, I have accomplished my goal and more. This is no longer a dream, it's my reality, and it's more than I ever wanted.

A few months later, I was still handling small cases and assisting other lawyers and paralegals. I was still waiting for my bar results and every day I grew more impatient. When I got back from lunch I checked my email, as I did every day. I gasped, attempting to catch my breath, the first email I saw was from the California State Bar. It was my bar results! I froze. I am excited for the results, but at the same time, they hold the key to my future. Keeping my job depended on me passing the bar. I realized it was now or... now. I counted down from three in my head and opened the email. I had to click the link and enter some information about myself. Once I did this, I had to scroll through all the names to find mine. There it was, Marcelo, Mariah; I passed! I was so excited, I screamed and instantly started crying. It was a long summer studying for the test, but I was so thankful to know all my hard work paid off. Not only did this mean I was able to stay at Parkers and Parkers Law Firm, but I would be promoted. I had to call my mom, dad, and sister to share the good news. I knew they would be excited for me as well. I ended my day early, I wanted to celebrate. So, I decided to drive to San Diego to celebrate with my sister for the weekend.

When I returned on Monday, I had a meeting with one of the partners. They congratulated me once again and showed me to my new office. They recently hired a new paralegal, and she would be working with me. Soon enough, I would have my own client list. I'm finally starting to feel like a real lawyer. When I first moved to Los Angeles, I didn't know what to expect. I felt like a small fish in a big pond. It was such a big city and there was so much I had to learn. The very first person I met was Krystal and it seemed like fate the way we met.

I was sitting at Joan's Deli, doing work, as I usually did on Wednesdays.

"Hi!"

I slowly raised my head to see a woman, who looked to be around my age standing there.

"Hello." I said back with a little hint of curiosity in my voice

"I see that you are here a lot, are you new to the city?"

"Yes, I am, how can you tell?" At this moment, I started to get nervous. Was she following me?

"You just have that look."

We both chuckled, she took the seat across from me, and there became our friendship.

Krystal had a slim build, brown skin with super curly and big hair. She was slightly taller than I was, about 5'4, with an even bigger personality. I noticed that the moment she came up to me. She was such a people person and had a way of bringing out the best in people.

She turned out to be a great friend. She was funny, outgoing, and a personal guide for me since I was new here in LA. I went to her in times of need or for someone to talk to, and she did the same to me. I enjoyed her company because it was easy to be myself around her. She didn't judge me nor my flaws and no matter what, we always had a good time. We clicked instantly and Krystal became like a sister to me. We would talk about everything from our childhood to our dating lives, or lack thereof in my case, and so much more. We also talked about growing up in church and reminisced about the church services we'd been to.

After truly getting settled into this new city, my job, and new house, I asked her if she knew of any good churches. That Sunday, I was on my way to Greater Pentecostal Church, GPC for short. I knew all about Apostolic Pentecostal Faith churches, as I grew up in one. I was excited to get back into the real groove of things. After attending service that Sunday, I decided to make myself a member. I genuinely enjoyed the music and the preaching. It reminded me so much of my church back home, I couldn't resist. It felt like I was home.

A few months passed and I was still enjoying the church. I couldn't wait to get back every Sunday to hear the word. One Sunday after service, I noticed a flyer. The church is looking for a new full-time pianist, with rehearsals two days a week at 5:00 p.m. After Krystal found out that I played piano and organ, she insisted that I go and audition, she pretty much forced me to go. I loved playing the piano and I knew that I could tear up a gospel song. I was pretty sure that it wouldn't interfere with work and I would love to play the piano again. She called me the night of the audition to let me know that she signed me up, I guess I didn't really have a choice now.

When I arrived at the church, I sat in my car to compose myself before heading into the church. I was super nervous, I didn't have much time to prepare since it was such short notice. I gave myself a little pep talk and then headed inside. Once I got to the front of the church, one of the deacons opened the door and shook my hand. He introduced himself as Deacon Patterson and let me know he would take me to the choir room. His smile was very warm, I guess it was obvious that I was nervous, as we walked, he placed a hand on my shoulder along with a reassuring smile. We enjoyed some small talk as we walked to the choir room and he told me not to be nervous. Everyone there was nice and loving and was excited to hear me play. I kept his kind words in the back of my mind throughout the entire audition. Before he walked away, he told me to break a leg and show them what I got.

When I walked into the choir room, I was greeted by the pastor, his assistant Daniel, the choir director Carl, the other pianist Emilio, and some of the other fellow saints and choir members. I was so nervous, I could barely think straight. I knew I shouldn't be thinking like this, but there was one person who caught my eye; The pastor. He was tall and handsome, and dressed simple. A blue t-shirt, black jeans, and white forces. The only clear thought I could formulate was, *white dude can dress.* I wasn't expecting him to look like this, compared to how he dressed on Sundays, suit and tie of course. But it was good to know he could dress outside of the formalness of the church.

Suddenly, my thoughts were interrupted.

"So, tell us a little about yourself." Carl asked.

Just when I thought I calmed down, my nerves resurface again. Tell me about yourself had to be one of the hardest questions to answer. I start with the basics, a formal introduction of myself. "Well, I recently moved here and a friend told me about this this church. I came one Sunday and never stopped.

They all shouted a little when I said that.

"I grew up in church, playing for my mom and my aunts. When I went off to college, I didn't have much time to play at church due to my major."

I was so nervous, I hope I wasn't talking too much. But everyone seemed interested, so I continued.

Finally, the time came for me to begin the real audition.

Carl asked if I knew how to play the organ.

"I learned when I was younger but I haven't played in a while." I responded.

"Oh, that's ok. We don't judge here, give it a try, let us hear something." Carl said.

I was so nervous, I couldn't even think of a song to play. I started out improvising until something popped in my head. I started with the melody to No Weapon by Fred Hammond, and followed it with Take It Back by Dorinda Clark Cole. Before I knew it, I was adding my own little touch along the way. One of the members started singing along and I instantly knew that was a plus.

After finishing the song, they all clapped and told me how good I was.

"How long have you been playing?" asked the pastor.

"Since the age of 6, my parents put me in training at that age." Ooooo's and ahhhhh's filled the room.

"Well Miss Mariah, sounds like you got the job." Carl said.

"OMG!!! Thank you so much." I said as I gave Carl and Pastor Matthew a hug.

"I hope that you know that this is a paying job. Would you prefer every two weeks or once a month?" Pastor Matthew asked.

I was so excited, I had to pause for a minute. "Ummm, once a month will suit me just fine."

"Okay then, see you next week. If I can just have your number and email address as I send weekly emails with links to songs and such for the choir to prepare for rehearsal" Carl said.

"Yes, you can. Sounds great!" I replied.

I waltzed out of that room with the biggest smile on my face, God has truly blessed me. I was filled with so much joy. I was able to do the two things I enjoyed the most, play piano in church and practice law. I couldn't be any happier. I had to call and tell my best friend the great news. Her reaction let me know that she was just as happy as I am, maybe even a little more. Today turned out to be a really great day!

Chapter 2:

My New Normal

Three more months passed, I was somehow managing work as a lawyer and two nights a week at the church. There were times that work would cause me to miss practices, but it didn't take long to show them I could handle everything, even with missing a few practices. Why? Because I was just that good, not to toot my own horn.

"Hey girl. What are you doing?" I said as soon as she answered.

"Oh, hey sweetie. Nothing much, I got off the phone with Daniel." she stated nonchalantly.

"Daniel? Like the pastor's assistant Daniel? You sure do talk to him a lot. He's a cutie." I was intrigued. I instantly wanted to know more on how she felt about him. I could tell she was blushing by the silence on the phone.

"Oh, stop it, haha, I mean I know he's cute and all but I don't think he'd date a girl like me." She replied, sounding defeated.

"Why wouldn't he? He'd be lucky to date a girl like you. You're pretty, smart, church going and you have a good head on your shoulders." I said. If I knew anything, I knew about doubting yourself before giving the opportunity a chance. No friend of mine was going to put themselves down on my watch.

"Well, I mean he doesn't seem interested. We talk and stuff but nothing more." She replied.

"Well maybe he's acting uninterested because you are." I said.

"Yeah. I don't know. Maybe we're supposed to be friends." She said.

"Show interest, I guarantee he'll show interest back." I replied back to her.

"Maybe you're right?" she stated as if she was thinking.

"I know I'm right. Hahaha." I said laughing.

Within the next few days, it seemed like fate. Daniel called Krystal and asked her on a date, of course she said yes. She was so excited, and I was happy for her too. Krystal and Daniel met a few years ago at the church. Oddly enough, they were both from Florida and even attended the same high school but never ran into each other. Daniel was one of the Pastor's first saints when he started the church and Krystal came shortly after. Their interest in each other grew swiftly. Since the church was small, it was easy to get to know people quickly.

Krystal loved that Daniel was simple. He was different from any other guy she dated. He didn't party or hang around the fast crowd. He wasn't very social, the exact opposite of Krystal. She was social and liked to hang out. She wanted to feel included and be in the know; Daniel was lowkey, he kept to himself and stayed out of trouble. They balanced each other out. Krystal would always tell me how welcoming Daniel was at the church. He always wanted to serve and help, which is why the Pastor made him the assistant early on. Krystal, being new in faith, really relied on others to carry her. She didn't know much about God or religion. But after many talks and bible studies with Daniel, her interest and love for God grew substantially. It also grew for Daniel. It was no shock to anyone when Daniel finally asked her out, they were almost inseparable. Before the date, Krystal was so afraid to show interest, thinking Daniel would do all the work. Even though I hadn't dated much or even had a boyfriend, one thing I knew is that guys like a chase. If they don't think you're worth their time, they won't try to "chase" after you. Once she showed interest, Daniel took to her like bait to a fish. Maybe that's all he was waiting for. Some type of signal or sign. I thought they looked so cute together.

Tuesday morning, I called Krystal to see if she wanted to have lunch, we needed to catch up and I wanted to hear all about her date.

"Hey chick!" I greeted her as I took my seat.

"Hey girl. What have you been up to lately?"

"You know, same ol' same ol'. Work and choir rehearsal."

"Oh ok. That's what's up. You really like playing the piano huh?"

"Oh yes. I love it! I mean, that was all I did when I was growing up. I couldn't wait to learn a new song so I could show it off to everyone." I said jokingly.

"Wow. That's so cool. I wish I knew how to play an instrument."

"Really? You still have lots of time."

"Yeah I guess so. But it's like people start at such young ages, so by the time they're 25 like me, they've mastered it."

"Well just because you've played for so many years doesn't mean you've got talent. You still have to practice and that will make up for all that lost time." I encouraged her.

"Yeah. That makes a lot of sense too. I'll think about it."

"So, tell me what's going on with you and Mr. Daniel? Huh?" I said glaring over my glass of water as I took a sip.

"What!" she said laughing, "Nothing, we talk and hang out and stuff like that."

"Well, how was the date?"

"The date was super laid back and casual, which was nice because it took the edge off. I think we were both really nervous."

"Where did you go? What did y'all talk about? Details please."

"We went to Chili's and had food and drinks. I really didn't think he drank because of the way he acts at church." She said laughing. "After he ordered one, I ordered one. Honestly, we sat there and laughed and talked more about our families and growing up. I found out he's from Florida like me. I wasn't expecting the date to go like that at all." her eyes lit up as she told the story.

"But why? You knew he liked you?"

"I mean I had an idea, but every time I saw him at church, he wouldn't speak much. We would always talk on the phone and text, which was weird. But, I have a good feeling he'll be speaking more now."

"Awe! You guys make such a cute couple." I replied back.

"Thanks girl. I really like him and I know he really likes me too. It could turn into something serious, but we're taking it slow for now."

"He seems like he makes you happy, which is really important."

"He really does, but enough about Mr. Daniel and I. Let's talk about you and Pastor Matthew."

"Umm. What about me and Pastor Matthew? I don't know him."

"Yeah. Well you don't have to. I see how you look at him. You better stop lusting, that man's a servant of God." she said jokingly.

"You know what? Only you'd say something like that." I said laughing "Yeah, I admit he's a very handsome man. He even caught my eye during the audition, but lust is out of the question. When would I have time to lust over any man? Especially him, I'd be too scared."

"Yeah you better… I'm just kidding. But, I have seen the way you smile at him. I think he likes you too. You know, I can find out." She said with a smirk.

"Krystal, don't go and do something stupid now. Everybody doesn't need to know my business. Yes, I think the pastor is handsome, but that's all it is and that's all it will be. Ok? End of topic."

"Ok. If you say so…" she ended.

As I was driving back to work, I couldn't stop replaying the end of our conversation back in my head. I wonder if he noticed me looking at him during the audition. Did he look back at me? I just hope Krystal keeps this conversation between us. She is known to run her mouth.
Like clockwork, Krystal called Daniel.

"Hey Daniel, what are you doing?" Krystal says.

"Hey sweet pea! Nothing, just sitting at home watching TV. And you?" Daniel replies.

"Ohhh nothing, I bet I know something that you'd like to know" Krystal said excitedly.

"Oooo. Do tell!" he said excitedly.

Krystal rarely calls Daniel without some type of small talk before the real conversation. But tonight, she got right to the point.

"Well you can't say anything to anyone, but I think Mariah likes Pastor Matthew." Krystal says.

"Wait, are you being serious, because the other day I somehow got him to admit that he loved her playing the organ and stuff and that he looked forward to it every Sunday." He replied.

"OMG! Really! This can't be happening. So, both of them like each other but neither of them knows." She screamed.

"Yep. Sounds like it to me. I think he's keeping it cool cause he doesn't really know her. He can't just go around dating random women and whatnot."

"Yeah I feel you on that. But Mariah is such a good girl; she doesn't date, talk to, or even bother to look at men." She said laughing "She's so consumed with work and church, she doesn't even miss it. She's truly a saved woman of God."

"Yeah. You can tell that by looking at her. I mean, they can at least date or something? Right? I mean there's no harm in getting to know each other. I'm sure if she did turn out to be a heathen or something that God will reveal that to him."

"Yeah babe. I agree with you, but you can't say anything. Mariah would kill me if she found out that I told you first."

They both agreed that they would keep this between them for now.

The next day I called Krystal to chat and immediately regretted telling her my thoughts about Pastor.

"You did WHAT!!!!" I screamed at Krystal

"Well I told Daniel and he said that Pastor Matthew liked you too. But I didn't think he was going to say anything to him. I told him not to." she said back.

"OMG Krystal! I told you not to say anything to anyone! Now this man is going to think something totally different about me and it's not true. I told you that in confidence. You're my best friend. I trusted you. Come on now." I said yelling into the phone.

"Look Mariah, I truly am really sorry. We were just talking and I was just going to leave it at that but then Daniel said Pastor liked you too, so I kept going. Please forgive me. Trust me, Pastor thinks the world of you, that won't change.

"Ugh! I can't stay mad at you forever but jeez, next time keep your mouth shut. Please, can you do that?"

"Yes, I can. I'm really sorry. It won't happen again. I promise." Krystal said, apologetically.

"Yeah, you better promise, jeez man", I ended the conversation I needed to wrap my head around all of this.

I couldn't believe Krystal ran and told Daniel what I thought about Pastor. Those two are like brothers, so of course Daniel would say something to him. Sometimes she blows me. I can't believe that just casually came up in their conversation. One-minute Matthew and Daniel are talking about football, the next they're talking about how much he likes me. How did Krystal manage to fit that into their conversation anyways? Ugh!

 Now things are going to be awkward around Pastor Matthew, he knows my biggest secret and it just so happens to be about him. Great! He's going to kick me out of the choir for committing fornication or something weird to make it less awkward. Thinking about this makes me sad now. If only Krystal could've kept her big mouth shut. I should've known though, that girl couldn't keep her mouth closed if you told her that it would cure world hunger and world peace. We'd all be doomed. I guess it's partially my fault too. Well there's no need to keep dwelling on it, I will just have to move on and hope nothing happens.

Chapter 3:

It Happens

Today was Wednesday, a court day. It would have been a normal Wednesday for me, if I didn't have the conversation I did last night with Krystal. I'm trying to keep my nerves under wraps, because I have court today, but I can't stop thinking about the fact that I have to go by the church later, and I'm scared I may run into… Pastor. I know I need to go pick up the music for next week's rehearsal, but I'm a little hesitant. But, I can't not get it. We have this church convention coming to town and I need to start reviewing the music, but ughhh… how can I face him?

After court, I went back to the office to finish some work. I have to head out a little early to get to the church in time before Pastor locks up. I can already feel the butterflies boiling in my stomach as time gets closer, *come on Mariah, shake it off*. I'm not sure if I'm more nervous because he knows I like him or because I know he likes me too. The last thing I want is for anything to be weird; I feel like the unpopular girl in high school gushing at the football star. I calm myself down before it's time to go.

The day seems to be dragging on, and I'm already tired. I decide to leave early and get some dinner before I head to the church. It was really just a stall, I couldn't wait any longer, I'll just have to deal with whatever happens. When I get to the church, I head straight to the choir room to pick up the three boxes Carl wanted me to get. I wanted to get in and out. Since they're fairly small boxes, I decided to carry them out to the car myself. Suddenly, some music falls off the top box and after realizing I probably should have asked for help, I turn around and see Pastor Matthew coming to give me a hand.

"Need a little help?" he asks, smiling.

"Thanks, it's been a long day." I reply, trying not to look too excited to see him.

"Everyone has those days, and with you being a lawyer, I'm sure it's more frequent for you." He replied looking up at me with a soft grin on his face, as he grabbed the boxes from me.

"They sure are." I started laughing, as I replied back. "Thanks for the help. I really appreciate it." I couldn't help but notice his perfect smile.

We continue to walk out to my car.

"Oh, you're most welcome. It's the least I can do, so that you keep blessing us with that music every Sunday." He replied, smiling again.

"Oh, that's nothing. Just something I love doing." We both smile. After a short awkward silence, I continue the conversation. "Well thanks, again. I should get going." I quickly turn to unlock my car.

"Ok, you're welcome. But, wait… wait… Ms. Marcelo, ummm, do you mind if I take you to dinner Friday at Le Lieu Du Déjeuner?" He asked me.

I paused before answering. "I love that restaurant. Sure, I suppose." Le Lieu Du Déjeuner is French for "The Lunch Spot". They served authentic French cuisine for lunch and dinner.

"How's 7pm? I'll meet you there, or I could pick you up? Whatever works best for you." He said as he put the boxes in my back seat.

I could hear the nervousness in his voice, but it's actually quite cute.

"Sounds good! We can meet there because I'll be getting off work around that time." I reply smiling.

"Okay, see you then! I hope you have a good night." He waits for me to get inside of my car before turning to head to his car.

I get in my car, trying to conceal the huge smile on my face; at least until he got to his car. I try my hardest to play it cool, but only God knows that it was only a matter of seconds before I burst out screaming with excitement. I was so happy, I could barely drive. I rush to get home so I can share the news with my sister Jhana.

"Jhana, you'll never guess what just happened!" I said to my sister on FaceTime.

"Girl what? Why are you screaming?" She said looking very puzzled. From the looks of things, she was having a spa night and I must have interrupted. She had a towel on her head, with a face mask, while trying to paint her toes.

"Because!" I said, pausing with excitement.

"Can you hurry up and say it already? I have a life to live." She motions with her hand, I can hear the irritation in her voice.
Jhana was so blunt, she didn't hold back for anyone and I loved it.

"Okay, okay, he asked me to dinner!" I started screaming again.

I couldn't help it, I told Jhana every detail of my life, and she did the same. She knew just as much as Krystal how much I liked Matthew.

"Shut up! You're lying! He really did?" Her excitement was matching mine now. She put the nail polish down, she was completely invested in my story

"Yes, yes, yes! We're going to dinner Friday, I'm so excited. I feel like a high school girl crushing on the star football player."

"Girl! Except the star football player is fine!" She yelled.

"Yes! I guess he was digging me all along."

"I tried telling you!" She said.

Jhana was my big sister and I looked up to her so much. She always gave the best advice and was literally one of the best listeners I knew. She was right about Matthew and I didn't want to believe her at first. I had been so stuck in my own head, thinking my time of finding someone wouldn't come and then this happens. She always said he would say something to me when the time was right.

We talked a little while longer, more about my date with Matthew, and catching up on each other's lives. She lived in San Diego, which wasn't too far but she was equally as busy as I was. She was a Pediatrician at one of the Children's Hospitals. She let me know that she is currently applying to be one of the board members of the hospital. This doesn't typically happen for individuals for her age, especially so early in their career. Jhana literally does any and everything she puts her mind to. She told me how one day she was sharing with a doctor some of her ideas on how to improve hospital staff morale, and increase the outpatient rate. After hearing her ideas, they felt that she would be a great addition to the hospital board, this way she'd be able to implement her ideas and improvements. She immediately started the application process. I'm so excited for her, I really hope she gets the position. We continued talking a bit before we both needed to get ready for bed.

Chapter 4:

Our First Date

I woke up the next morning still on a high, I couldn't wait for Friday to come. I was so excited; I had to call Krystal and share the news with her.

"Hey Boo!" She answers the phone.

"Hey girl! I gotta tell you something." I replied.

"Is it what I think it is?" She asked.

"Umm, I don't know what you think it is, but he asked me out to dinner."

"Really?! I told you that he worshiped the ground that you walked on." She said excitedly.

"Shut up, that's not why I called you. I'm so nervous, like what should I wear? Should I wear what I wear to work, or take a change of clothes? Help me out!" I was starting to panic.

"Well, your work clothes are just as formal as you wearing a dress or something, because you always be looking fly.", she said laughing, "I say just wear your work clothes. Since you'll be getting off work you won't have much time to change. You'll still look cute. It's just dinner, right?"

"Yes, duh! But I still want to look good and stuff, you know?"

"Don't worry, you will." She assured me.

"Okay girl, let me get through this day so I can go on my date tomorrow!" I said, getting excited again.

"Okay, but you better call and tell me what happens. I want to know everything, no details left out."

"Okay, okay. I got you. Bye!" I said hanging up the phone.

I pulled into the parking lot of Le Lieu Du Déjeuner. I didn't want to seem too excited, but my heart was racing, a mix of excitement and nervousness. As I walked to the front door of the restaurant, I immediately felt overwhelmed with emotions. Nervous was an understatement. I was extremely excited but couldn't help but think if I should be doing this. I could instantly hear Jhana in my head, "Why would you think that? You deserve this!". In my world, there is no such thing as fate, so I must be here for a reason. I could hear faint jazz music seeping through the door, as I opened the door to step inside. I instantly knew the tune, it was "Ruby, My Dear", by the famous Thelonious Monk. The room smelled of steak and a variety of cheeses. I let the host know that I was meeting someone; I scanned the room and spotted him at a table near the back of the room. When I got to the table, he rose from his seat to greet me with a hug. After I took my seat he pushed my chair in. I couldn't help but notice how good he looked. He was sporting a navy-blue suit, with a white button up shirt, and a navy-blue striped tie to match. What a coincidence, I wore the same colors. Once we both sat down, he immediately started the conversation.

"Hello. How are you?" He asked.

"I'm doing great actually, I'm a little tired, but I'll make it."
I replied back.

"How was your day?" he asked.

"It was pretty nice, just court, that's about it Pastor."

"Please, you can call me Matthew; we're not at church." He said smiling.

"Oh, ok…Matthew." I was shocked at how candid and straightforward he was. "How was your day?"

"It was fairly nice, sort of busy, but not too bad."

"That's good to hear."

Our waitress came and introduced herself, and took our drink orders. I still needed time to look over the menu, and I can't lie I was enjoying just talking.

"So, tell me a little bit more about yourself?" He asked.

"Well, I'm 25 years old, I moved here for college to get my law degree. In the beginning of my last year of school, I was offered an internship at Parker and Parkers Law Firm. Working there helped me to finish my degree faster, along with taking summer classes. After I graduated, I was offered a job and I've been working there for about two and a half years. Umm, let's see, what else? My mom and dad live back in Denver, along with my brother Cameron. My sister Jhana lives in San Diego. I grew up in the church, so that's the one thing that I really know well. What about you?"

"Well, I'm also 25 and I've lived here for about six years. I transferred from NYU to finish up my degree in Accounting and Business. I'm an accountant at South Branch Bank downtown and I also do some work at the North Branch too. I'm from Chicago. I also have a younger brother named Jordan and an older sister named Eden."

"How long have you been a pastor?" I asked.

"Only for about three years now. My father is a pastor in Chicago. Many would say that I'm following in his footsteps but I never imagined myself being a pastor. I guess God had a different calling for my life. I started with a small congregation, and soon enough they started telling their friends who spread the word about a new church expanding and so on. We started in a storefront, but quickly outgrew that. So, my dad agreed to help me start building my own church. We've been at the church for almost two years now. It was a hard start at the beginning, but with prayer and faith, I didn't give up because I knew I had to fulfill the plan God has for me."

"Wow, that's amazing. It's really something to try to plan out our lives, then God decides that he wants something different for us. At that point there is nothing we can do but follow."

"You know, that is so true. Honestly, becoming a pastor is the best thing that I could have ever done. I get so much done, I get to help people, serve God constantly, and have a closer relationship with him."

"You are a true man of God."

"I appreciate that. All I do is for God alone. Now tell me some more about your job. What is it like being a lawyer?"

"Well…", I said laughing. "It's not an easy job at all, there's a lot that has to be done and communication is key with your team. Especially between you and your paralegal. It requires a lot of late nights and sometimes early mornings. It's not as bad in between cases. Then, it's just filling out papers and preparing for the next case. When court time rolls around, the stress and pressure is really high. I have to really be on top of things, and sometimes it's hard getting enough sleep; or at least for me it is, with all the anxiety. No one likes an exhausted lawyer during trial."

"It does sound like a lot."

"Don't get me wrong, I love what I do, but it's also a lot to handle."

"What made you become a lawyer?"

Before I could answer, our waitress came back to check on us, but I think she could tell we were enjoying the conversation, she said she would give us a little more time.

I continued. "I love watching Law and Order. Watching them solve cases excited me. I would say to myself, I'd love to do that one day. It was really interesting to me. As I got more involved in the field, I liked it more and more. It just drew me in and I loved it. What made you become an accountant?"

"Well, mainly because I really like math and I wanted to work in a field where I could make a decent amount of money. So, accounting seemed like the perfect choice and I actually really like."

"That's really nice. I love math too, ironically. So, what exactly do you do?"

"I'm a public accountant. I help people and businesses to file and pay taxes on time, I also help them manage their finances, sort of like financial advising. At North Branch, I also handle some government accounting which includes helping and examining local government records, finances, and taxes. I do that with a group of people twice a month."

"Okay, sounds nice, "businessman"." I say as I take a sip from my drink.

"Yeah, a lot of my clients actually go to the church. A lot of my business comes from them."

"That's good, that you have a decent client list.

"So, I have a question?"

"Yeah?" I say kind of nervously.

I felt my stomach drop to my toes. What was he about to ask?

He leans in a little. "Were you expecting me to ask you out sooner?" he looks down.

"Honestly, yes, well really hoping. It was awkward walking around pretending we didn't know each other's secrets. I wasn't really sure if you were interested until the day before you asked me to dinner. What took you so long?" I chuckled, jokingly.

"I guess I set myself up for that one."

I noticed his face turned red and he was blushing. He was even cuter now.

"Well, honestly. I really wanted to see what you were about first. But, Krystal and Daniel didn't make the job any easier. I didn't want to rush things and I had to make sure you were actually into me."

"Did you not believe them?" I asked.

"Well, Krystal is known to exaggerate a little. She has wanted me to be with someone for a while. "What's a pastor with no first lady?" He mimicked Krystal. Who knew if this was just a scheme or not."

"Krystal is definitely a character to say the least, but I think she means well. Well, I'm glad you finally got the courage to ask"

I couldn't help but start blushing myself. The waitress comes back to take our order.

"Order whatever you want.", he says smiling.

I couldn't stop blushing. I ordered a shrimp pasta with special sauce and he ordered filet mignon. She wrote our orders down and said she'd be right back with more wine. Our conversation continued.

"If you really want the rundown, I've been watching you since you came in for that audition. I remember it like it was yesterday. You looked beautiful with your long black hair. And then you started playing, and I was blown away, I knew you were special then. I thought it was a little "kiddish" how everything came about with Krystal and Daniel. I really would have preferred to start the conversation myself. But at the same time, it lit some fire under my butt." He started laughing.

I couldn't help but think, if you want me to marry you, just say that. Real smooth talker. I was speechless and that doesn't happen very often. Could he get any more amazing at this point? We were silent after this, as we both finished our meals. But not the awkward silence you want to run away from. Oddly, this silence made me lean into him even more. I couldn't help but realize how empty the restaurant had gotten. I glanced down at my watch and noticed how late it was.

"Wow, I didn't realize that it was so late." I say surprised, checking my phone.

"Oh wow. Yes, it is late. I guess we should be leaving huh?"

"Yeah. I've got to get up early and head to the office to finish up some work for court Monday."

"Well I know you have an early morning tomorrow. I'll let you head home." He says raising from his chair and walking over to mine.

"Alrighty then. I really enjoyed myself, the conversation was great. Thanks for a great time."

"You're welcome, I enjoyed myself also. Perhaps dinner or something else again?"

"I'd like that."

"Great."

Like a gentleman, he walked me to my car and hugged me goodbye. I didn't know why I was shocked by this notion. He helped me with my chair, held the door open, and made sure I was safely in my car before he walked away. I guess, it's just not that common anymore.

I got into my car, leaving the parking lot as I watched him walk away. I couldn't believe what an educated man he was, and he truly loved God. That was a definite plus for me. I am already looking forward to that next date!

Saturday morning came all too quick. I couldn't even focus on what was going on. I really needed to get this work done for this upcoming case I had. But I couldn't seem to keep my mind off of Matthew. What is this? I've never felt this way about a man before. I mean, is this wrong? I know he's a man of God and all but I think I'm becoming attracted to him. He's really sweet and he really knows how to have a great conversation. It seemed like we talked the entire time, and I never got bored. The date kept replaying in my head, is this the butterflies feeling that people talk about. As soon as he told me to call him Matthew, it seemed my nerves escaped me. This has been one of my best dates, in such a long time. A few moments later, I get a call from Krystal.

"Hey girl. What's new with you?" Krystal says to me.

"Nothing just at work sitting here." I reply.

"Well, since you're at work, don't you need to be doing some work? Haha." She said laughing.

"Yeah, I suppose so. I got a lot on my mind though."

"Like?"

"Last night."

"Oh yeah. Dinner with the Pastor. So, tell me, what happened?"

"I don't know. You may go back and tell Daniel." I say sarcastically.

"Come on. Don't do me like that. I won't say anything to him, I promise. Well, being that Pastor hasn't already told Daniel, you tell me", she says laughing.

"Well, okay I guess." I'm actually excited to tell her. "So, it was the best night of my life. We went to Le Lieu Du Déjeuner, ate and chatted all night, basically until the place was about to close."

"Wow. Really? What did y'all possibly talk about all that time?"

"Like everything! How we grew up, church, family life. I even mentioned me being the head of a bike gang me and my cousin were in. I was a complete nerd as a child." I laughed a little. "He got a real kick out of that."

"A bike gang? What?" She laughed back.

"Yes girl. I was maybe 10 or 11 and my cousin was five or six and we hung out with girls around the neighborhood. We all had bikes and would ride different places, to the store, the library, and the park. We called ourselves, "Girls on Bikes" and I was the leader since I was the oldest. He told me I was bossy."

I began to laugh again, thinking about those childhood stories.

"Wow, bossy huh. You're going to give him a run for his money. So, what else did yawl talk about?"

"Well we talked about him growing up as a preacher's kid and all the pressure he constantly felt to be "good". He told me him and his sister handled the pressure better than his brother, it caused him to rebel. We talked about him being a pastor, his job, my job, and our parents. I mean we talked about literally everything under the sun. I've never talked to anyone like that before."

"Rebel, sounds like my kind of guy", she said mischievously. "But awe. That's really sweet. He seems like he's a sweet guy and all. I'm glad that you had a good time with him, but you need to get back to work. I don't want you complaining to me about how you gotta leave service early because you didn't want to do any work today and you have to do it all tomorrow. We can talk after church."

"Okay okay, I'm going now. Bye girl!"

"Tell me more tomorrow!" She ended the conversation.

Chapter 5:

Wow... Slow Down

Sunday morning came and I was excited, this is the first Sunday I was up before my alarm, but when it finally went off I jumped out of bed startled. I was ready to get to church, but it seemed for all the wrong reasons. Don't get me wrong I am always excited to go to church, but today I had a little extra excitement. I had to slow down and catch myself, realizing what I was doing and why. Is it wrong for me to keep thinking about him? I mean, the date was nothing short of amazing; he's smart, kind, loves God, and most of all handsome. The way he spoke, with such presence. I immediately sensed he knew who he was, he's confident, not too cocky, but very sure of his place. He genuinely cares about people, which I love, I can't stop replaying the date in my head. The food, atmosphere, and conversation was nearly perfect. I can still hear the music faintly in the background playing under our conversation as we learned more and more about each other. I'm not sure what to expect, especially with him being a Pastor. I can't remember the last time I went on a date, as bad as that may sound. I just don't want to rush into anything, but I genuinely like this guy. He gave me butterflies from the first time I saw him.

"Bum, Bum, Bum, Bum." I wake to the blaring sound of my alarm clock. Iphone's classic "radar" sound always gets me out of bed. The last few days, all I could think about was Mariah. The way we were able to talk for hours, and it only seemed like 30 minutes. I can have a conversation with her forever. My favorite thing about her is her organ playing. I've never heard someone play with such grace and so effortlessly. When she gets on that organ or keyboard, people in the church instantly get saved all over again. Only God can make her sound the way she does, and she knows that. At her audition a few months ago, when she walked in, I could instantly feel the presence of God walking with her. I still remember it, like it was yesterday. She walked in wearing a long-sleeved jumper with white converse chucks, the classics. I couldn't tell if she was nervous or not because she had such a calm demeanor to her. She seemed so confident and knew what she came there to do. When she started playing, I instantly knew it was Dorinda Clark-Cole. The way she made the song her own without making it unrecognizable. She plays with such compassion and feeling. She can bring you into the song with her, and you feel what she's feeling while playing. I can't wait to get to church so I can hear her play again.

After service, a few members greeted me.

"Oh, Sister Mariah, that song you played today was wonderful. Let's get back to Eden, living on top of the world. Isn't that song the truth? I love your playing, anointed woman of God. Be blessed baby girl." Mother Massy said to me as I waited in the foyer for Krystal.

I responded with a simple nod of the head and a thank you as she continued to walk past.

"Marvelous praise service today sister." Another member said.

"Thank you brother, God bless you." I replied.

While I waited for Krystal to come out of the sanctuary, various members walked by and stopped to chat. Even though I was waiting for Krystal, I secretly hoped Matthew would walked by. I wonder if anyone can tell how distracted I am. I kept looking over everyone's shoulder in hopes of seeing Matthew. I almost broke my nail rushing out of the house just to make sure I got to church on time. I didn't want to miss a minute of his preaching. I got so caught up in my head daydreaming about us, I almost missed Krystal coming out of the sanctuary hand in hand with of course, Daniel.

"Earth to Mariah!"
I hear someone yell from across the room, that girl could stop a stampede of elephants with her voice. I snap out of my daydream to see Krystal and Daniel approaching me hand in hand.

"You want to get lunch with me today so we can talk?" I say to Krystal, hinting that I just want it to be us so we can finish talking about the date.

"Ummm, I'm sorry it's our anniversary today and I totally forgot. I had to play it off like I knew even though I didn't." She leaned into whisper to me. "He wants to take me to dinner and stuff. I hope you're not mad or anything." She replies.

"No, go ahead girl and enjoy yourself. I'll probably just go home and cook for myself."

"I love you lots and I promise I'll make it up to you."

We parted our separate ways and my mind started to whirl again.

I waited a little longer for Matthew to come out of the sanctuary, but he was nowhere to be found. I wondered if he was looking for me as well. I stuck around and spoke to a few more of the church members, hoping he'd appear, trying to hide the excitement and emotion on my face. I was trying so hard to keep my feeling under wrap, I didn't want anyone to know what was going on. At least, until we figured out what exactly we wanted. Once I finished talking to the last of the saints, I decided to call it and go home. I didn't want anyone to notice me standing around and ask who I was waiting for. Especially with Krystal being gone, I didn't have a cover story.

When I arrived home, I started cooking dinner. I decided to cook fettuccine alfredo with baked chicken. It was a quick and easy meal. It was still bothering me that I didn't get to speak with Matthew when church was over. I guess you could say I missed him. I waited around for 15 or 20 minutes, but I never saw him. Maybe he just got caught up with something. I haven't spoken with him since yesterday when he texted me good morning and to have a good day at work. Had he forgotten about me? Should I call him or wait? My mind started to wonder, and I began to get ahead of myself. I didn't want to jump to any conclusions, it was still too early. I also don't want to seem too clingy and not give him enough space. One thought, I didn't ask him if he was seeing someone else. I just assumed he wasn't since he took me to dinner, or at least I hope he'd tell me if there was. A pastor wouldn't date multiple people at once, would they? Maybe I'm overreacting, times like these I really need Krystal.

After I finished cooking dinner, I decided to take a much-needed nap. After creating all those scenarios in my head, I wore myself out.

When I got up, a few hours had passed and I saw I had a few missed calls from my parents, sister, and Matthew. I instantly jumped up and my heart started beating fast. I'd been waiting to hear from him. I was so excited and needed time to calm down, I'll call him last. I had to fill my sister in on the latest news about what was happening and reassure my dad that I was doing okay out here in this "big city, all by myself" as he would put it.

"Hey, sorry I missed your call. I was taking a nap." I said over the phone to Matthew.

"It's ok. I didn't get to speak to you after service. By the time I came out, you were already gone, and I didn't see your car in the parking lot. I had to speak to a few members after service." He said.

"Yeah, Krystal and I were supposed to go to lunch, but something came up, so I just decided to go home." I left out the part where I stayed and waited for him.

"Oh ok. I wanted to tell you how I enjoyed your playing today. Donald Lawrence is actually one of my favorite gospel artists. I love his songs."

"Me too. He does some pretty different things in the Gospel world, but in a good way."

"How long does it take you to learn a song?"

"Well it just depends on how much time I spend on it really. If I just sit down and learn the whole thing right then and there, it takes like maybe two hours or so, maybe less. Something to that nature. I've never really counted. But usually I don't sit and learn the whole song in one sitting." I chuckled. "So maybe like a couple of days. I also like changing some of the chords I hear because I may not like how they sound in the song, so I make it a little more interesting and what not, adding my own touch."

"Wow. That's amazing. Carl says when you come to rehearsal, you only know half or part of a song."

"Yeah", I said laughing. "That's true. It's not because I don't have time. It's just that we usually never go over the whole song the first time anyways and sometimes I just don't feel like finishing it. I always know it well enough so that if we do get past the part I didn't learn, I can still follow along."

"Ok. I can understand that. What are you doing? Are you busy or anything?"

"I'm just eating. I'm not busy."

"Oh ok, good. So, tell me something interesting, that not a lot of people know about you?""

Wow I'm shocked at his question and his intrigue to get to know me more, maybe he is really interested, and not seeing anyone else.

"Well, my grandfather and my dad served in the military for some years."

"Really? What service and for how long?"

"Well, I'm not exactly sure how long my grandfather served in the Army. I know that my dad was an Army brat and he hated it. He literally had to move almost every year until he was about six years old. That's when my grandfather unlisted and moved here to the states until my dad went off to college. Then, they moved back to China. Umm, my dad served in the Navy for three years. He served a year, met my mom and married her, left for another year, came back and had my brother, and then he left for another year and that was it. He didn't want my mom and brother to have to move all the time like he did, so he always made sure he came home on his leaves."

"Wow, I think that is really cool. Did either of them fight in any particular wars?"

"Yeah, my grandfather actually fought in the Korean War."

"Wow, I would have never guessed that."

"Anything interesting about you or your family?"

"Well, no one fought in any wars or anything like that, but both my dad and I were Valedictorian in high school. And I graduated top of my class in both Undergrad and Graduate school."

"Wow, so you're super smart huh?"

"I guess you could say that," he replied laughing "Tell me more about your brother and sister."

"Ok. Well my brother Cameron is the oldest he just turned 30, and he's an architect. He studies older buildings from different countries and then draws blueprints for new buildings incorporating some of the older buildings' structures. Then it's my sister Jhana. She's a pediatrician at the Children's Hospital in San Diego. She just turned 27 and then me, I'll be 26 next month. What about yours?"

"First, it's my sister Eden, she's 29, she's a contract lawyer. Then me, and then my younger brother Jordan who is 23. He's finishing up his degree in Elementary Education. Can I ask you a question?"

"You just did." I say laughing.

"Ok, well another one."

"Yeah" I say, still laughing.

"Are you prepared for court tomorrow?"

"Yes, but very nervous. I'm working on a big case right now."

"Really, what is it about?".

"What type of lawyer are you?"

"A defense attorney. But I also do some work at the DA's office."

"Oh ok. What's the case about?"

"Well, I can't tell you much or I could go to jail", I say smiling, "but it's a murder case that you've probably heard about on the news with that man that supposedly killed that little girl and her mom."

"Oh yeah, that guy Sam something. I have heard of that. They did say on the news that a lawyer from Parker and Parkers Law Firm had the case, but I never would have guessed it was you."

"Yeah. I'm defending him on one count sexual assault on a minor, 2nd degree murder, involuntary manslaughter, and failure to show up at his arraignment. But he did commit the latter."

"Wow. He has it in for himself huh? And you're supposed to get him off?" he asks curiously.

"Yeah. I was lucky enough to get it. It was one of those cases where it wasn't assigned to a specific lawyer. It's kind of like whoever wants it or isn't currently working on a case gets it. It was passed down from the DA's office."

"Do you think he did it?"

"Honestly, no I don't. This man just so happens to be black and the girl and her mother were white. I'm actually really surprised the judge allowed the case to proceed because the Plaintiff side didn't have very much evidence but a witness that supposedly saw a black man, described as my client leaving the house with the murder weapon. It has not been proven if this witness is liable or not and they couldn't point him out from a lineup. So that is something that I will bring up in court. I'm pretty confident that I can get him off."

"But how do you know for sure he didn't do it?"

"Well, I can sense it. And he has a strong alibi with witnesses and two videos shots of him at work, so I think it's going to be hard placing him at the scene of the crime. I also take time to pray about the cases I get so I make the right decision when going in. But since it's a battle between races, they'll make a case on something."

"Well, good luck with that and I will be praying that you have strength to get through all of this. Wait one more question?"

"Shoot."

"Say you don't win this whole thing and he has to go to jail. How long would he have?"

"Life without parole."

"Wow..." He sounded shocked.

"Exactly. So, I have to do all I can to prove he's innocent."

"I have faith in you. You can do it." he says smiling.

"Thank you." I say smiling back. "I'm still nervous because I'm not sure what exactly I've gotten myself into." His words were reassuring.

"Well of course I did. What do you mean? It can't be that bad, can it?"

"It's not that it's bad. It's just really nerve-wrecking. Especially since this guy has a lot going against him and I know that I'd be really sad if he had to go to jail for a crime that he didn't commit. It also angers me that innocent men can go to jail so easily, when there are real murderers and rapists roaming the world. I guess it's just the fact that so much points to him being not guilty, but I'm just really worried about the whole "race" card."

"Here's what I'm going to tell you. I believe that you can do it. You know what? You're a good lawyer and that's why you were chosen, right? If it really turns out that this guy didn't commit the crime, justice will prevail, no matter the race or evidence they may think they have against him. Everything will work out. You must have faith and believe."

"You make it sound so easy. Haha. If only it was though."

"Well, I don't know much about being a defense attorney except what you've told me, but I'm sure that you're going to do everything in your power to get him off. I also know that you believe in God and he can help you do any and everything you want to do. Right?"

"Yes, that is true. He definitely can. I will do all that I can. It's just that I've never felt like this before about any case. Maybe because there's a lot riding on this one, in terms of his life. I'll be ok, hopefully."

"As long as you're ready, everything will be okay. I know this." he says.

"Oh, and how do you know this?"

"I just do. Say a prayer before you go to bed and before the case tomorrow. God's got you."

"Ok, well I'm going to believe and hope that you're right."

"I am. You should get you some rest before tomorrow. Yeah?"

"Yeah. I should. I have to look over some paperwork and a few other things before tomorrow."

"Okay, well I'll let you go and I'll call you tomorrow to see how everything went."

"Sounds like a plan."
I paused for a moment remembering the conversation I had in my head from earlier.

"Wait, one more thing. I never asked you if you were seeing someone." I was hoping it didn't get awkward on the phone and he said what I wanted to hear.

"Actually, Yes I am."

"Oh." I replied, feeling my heart drop. "I didn't know."

"Well, you should, because it's you." He replied.
I wasn't even sure what to say. I wasn't expecting that answer either.

"Goodnight Mariah."

"Goodnight Matthew." I replied, still a little speechless.

I wake up to soaked pajamas. It was 5:30am, 30 minutes before the loud buzzing of my alarm. I noticed the sheets are overturned from all the tossing I did last night. My scarf is lying next to me on the pillow and I'm missing one sock. All last night I dreamt that Sam, the guy I'm defending, went to jail serving three life sentences. When I look in the mirror, I realize I'll have to take the extra time to hide the bags under my eyes. No one wants a half-asleep lawyer. As I got ready to head to court, I kept hearing Matthew's words that everything was going to go well and it would be okay. With each thought came a smile. He's so reassuring. And with that, I went to work.

Court didn't go as bad as I thought. The judge threw out the plaintiffs' eyewitness because she failed to point my client out in a line up and she was diagnosed with being senile. So that's a definite plus. If they can't find any other witnesses or evidence putting my client at the scene of the crime, the case will be thrown out due to lack of evidence. Which saves me a lot of time, effort, and the state a lot of money.

I realize it's 1 o'clock I've been in court all day. It was around lunch time and I decided to call Matthew to see if he was free to go to lunch. After our conversation last night, I gained more confidence, because I've never been one to initiate things.

He answers after a couple of rings.

"Hey, want to have lunch or something? I'm done with court today and I don't have any work to do at the office." I ask nervously, quickly recognizing I jumped right into the ask.

"Sure, where?" he says.

"How about Applebee's?" I ask.

"Okay, sounds good to me. Meet you there in about 30 minutes and we can talk about your day at court?" he says.

"I can't wait." I hung up the phone, having the biggest smile on my face. My day instantly got better.

Every time I'm with him, I just feel this natural high. He makes me laugh and he's sweet, and just so smooth but in a good way. The way he said he was seeing me last night on the phone when I asked him if he was seeing someone. I definitely wasn't expecting that. I was glad and shocked when I heard those words. I hoped there was no one else, he's basically any and everything I could ask for in a man. I know God really loves me because he allowed me to meet Matthew. I mean not only does he make me feel good on the inside, but I love it when that man preaches. When he brings the word, he brings it and makes sure you get it through your head and understand it. I could go on and on about him, there's just so much to say. It's hard to sum everything up into words.

—

I think it's safe to say she thinks about me just as much as I think about her. It's funny, just when I'm thinking about how she's doing, she calls me. It's like we're in sync with each other. Is that possible just after a few conversations? Maybe it is really meant to be, but only time will tell.

Chapter 6:

The Proposal

They say time flies when you're having fun, and that's the case with Matthew and I. I can't believe it's really been nine months already, our relationship has blossomed into something so organic, it still feels unreal. It's almost frightening how natural it feels. Nothing was forced, and most of all, I feel safe with him. I find myself falling in love with this man more and more every day. The feeling is indescribable. Imagine, finding someone you click with, you don't have to pretend with them, you don't have to try to be anything or anyone else with them. They just seem to understand you. You instantly melt when they are around and their arms become your safe haven. When you feel it, you just know? Every Friday, we go out on dates and try different restaurants. But sometimes, we still visit our favorite Le Lieu Du Déjeuner. We stay up late talking on the phone, we email and text during the day. He still surprises me for lunch dates and sometimes he'll just drop by and bring me food and flowers. We're slowly integrating ourselves into each other's world and revealing what goes on behind the scenes of our lives. Some days, he'll come over and we'll do work together. He shows me some of the things he does to keep the church running properly and how he prepares for services every week, I enjoy this the most. I know how passionate he is about his ministry, and I feel honored to be included in any way possible. It shows that he trusts me. We go volunteer together and sometimes when he's free, he comes to court to watch me in action. We're always hand in hand in church, and now some of the saints are starting to wonder what's really going on with us. Our relationship is still young and fresh, and still figuring things out. I wonder if it'll become a problem for them, at least I hope it won't. We're taking things slow, to ensure we maintain our faith and principals. It's nice having someone around that genuinely cares about you and makes you feel special and wanted.

—

The last few months with her have been nothing short of amazing. I've really spent time getting to know Mariah and she's unlike any girl I've met. Anytime I think about her, my day instantly becomes brighter. Even though it's only been a few months, things are starting to get real. I'm considering spending the rest of my life with this woman. I thought it would be a good idea to call my dad to get some advice about marriage and proposals. I've always looked up to my parents' relationship and wanted to be like them some day. With him being a pastor as well, I knew he'd have some good advice for me.

"Hey dad. How's it going?"

"Hey son. Your mother and I were just talking about you."

"Oh yeah? What about?" I asked. I hope it was something good.

"Oh, just how all of you kids are doing. Eden has a great job and she's happy. Jordan finally got his degree and is doing well. And you."

"And me what?" I say laughing.

"You're dating that beautiful girl. What's her name again?"

"Mariah." I replied. I couldn't help but smile saying her name. I was happy hearing my dad talk about us It was the perfect Segway into my question.

Yes, Yes, Mariah. That's her!" He said excitedly.

"Well that's exactly why I was calling. I think she might be the one dad. How do I know for sure?"

"That's such a great question, one that everyone asks. But honestly son, there's no answer that I can give you. Only you will know when the right one comes along. Pray and ask God for clarity."

"Well, I have prayed about us a lot." I said laughing. "Our relationship has progressed so much in the last nine months. I've never felt like this about anyone else. I just don't want to feel like I'm rushing into anything." So many thoughts began to flood my head.

"The only person that can make that decision is you. I can't tell you if you're rushing into anything because I honestly don't know. Everyone's timeline is different. Some get married after dating for five years, some get married after dating for five months. You date someone until you feel like you know them enough to determine if they're worth the time and effort of spending the rest of your life with. Once you've made that determination, there's your answer."

"That makes sense, thanks dad. I know exactly what to do."

I hung up the phone knowing I'd made my decision. I had one more person to talk to before the time came.

"Hi, is this Jhana?" I called Mariah's sister. I needed her help.
"Umm, who is this?" she replied. She sounded upset.
"This is Matthew..."

"Matthew!" she screamed.

"Yes." I chuckled." I'm sorry to bother you but I really need your help. I got your number from Mariah's phone."

"Is everything okay? What's going on?" Her tone told me I getter get to the point.

"Yes, everything is fine. I actually wanted to know when you'd be coming to LA again?"

"Probably in the next few weeks. Why?

"I want you to help me pick out a wedding ring."

"No way! Are you serious? You're going to marry my sister. Like for reals? I am so excited!" She was now screaming and I had to pull the phone away from my ears.

"Yes, I've made my decision, I love her. I want to spend the rest of my life with her."

"Just let me know and I'll be there!" She said excitedly. "I still can't believe this, and you want my help with the ring? Matthew you are alright with me." She said laughing. "She will be so happy. I know how much she loves you." She followed.

"Thank you so much Jhana! I love her so much. I can't wait! Have a good day." I said as we both hung up.

—

It's been two weeks since we last saw each other. Even though we talk on the phone, it's still not the same. A last-minute trip to Atlanta pulled me away for much longer than expected. It was finally Saturday night and I was on my way back home. Church is tomorrow and Matthew and I will be reunited. I can honestly say I cannot wait for the day when I won't have to miss him as much. I didn't think I'd ever say this, but I'm in love with him and I wouldn't mind spending the rest of my life with him.

—

Last night seemed to draw out forever as I waited for Mariah to text me that she landed. I insisted on picking her up, but she said she parked her car at the airport, so there was no need. It was well after midnight when I finally got the text. I couldn't wait to see her at church tomorrow. Today is going to be "The Big Day" and she had no idea. I was able to get her to admit her ring size a few weeks ago while we were shopping. I think just before service ends, I'll call her up to the altar and pop the question. I got my best friends Daniel and Carl to be in on it as well.

I've been thinking about this for two months now. I wanted to be sure it was the right timing and the right person. I prayed and fasted, asking God to reveal to me if I was supposed to be with her. It's like he gave me every sign that she was the right one. Her sister even came down to see it all unfold. While Mariah was out of town, I drove to San Diego to meet her sister and buy the ring. I had an idea of what I wanted but what better person is there to get their approval. Even though Jhana is Mariah's sister, they're also best friends, almost the same person. I even call them twins. Jhana loved the ring so I know Mariah will too.

I spent my morning running around the house, completely absorbed in today's activities. Relieved I wasn't preaching today, I scattered the closet to find a suit, something just right for the occasion. I wanted everything to be perfect for her. I gave the ring to Carl a few days ago because I didn't trust myself not to forget it the day of. Once I finally settled on a suit, I rushed out the door. I got to the church earlier than normal, just to give myself time to calm down before everyone got there. As I pull up to the church lot, my heart began to beat even faster. After today, my life will change forever. But I'm so ready to welcome that change. I open the church doors and do my morning rounds to keep my mind off of things. Afterwards, I make some coffee and sit in my office for the last hour before church starts. I hope she will say yes.

—

Sunday morning arrives like the horses busting out of the gate at the Kentucky Derby. My head feels like it's glued to the pillow, as I try lifting it up to get ready for church. I feel my body slowly warming up as I contemplate staying home today. I've set an expectation and I know they're expecting me to play today, but mentally I am not up for it. A part of me wants to stay home in bed but the guilt quickly settles in, and I make my way to the shower to get dressed.

The drive to church was less than exciting, as I replayed the chords in my head for praise and worship. I arrived at church 20 minutes late, but still thankful I made it at all. Familiar faces greet me at the door, excited to see me after two weeks of absence. It was starting to settle in how much of an impact my playing was making. After a somewhat dreadful morning, seeing how much everyone's face brightened up made my entire attitude change. When I walk into the sanctuary, the first face I see is my sister sitting next to Krystal. "What are you doing here?", I mouth shocked. "I came to surprise you. Surprise!", she whispers to me. Lord knows how much I love my sister. Whatever the reason she's here, I'm excited, she can pop up anytime. I sit down next to Krystal, enjoying a few moments before praise service.

I spot Matthew in the pulpit and give him a smile as he returns one to me. He looks so good today. Beige suit, with a white shirt, peach colored tie, and white sneakers. Throughout the service, I glance over at him, he has this huge grin on his face. I'm wondering what he's thinking about because he doesn't look too interested in what the assistant pastor is preaching. After the sermon, he gets up to give his final remarks. But this time, he says he has an announcement.

"Well church, this is going to be a big day for me. I have an announcement to make. Can I ask Mariah to come down to the altar please?" Pastor says.

I walk down the stairs from the organ to where Matthew is standing. I'm confused as to why he calls me to the front of the church. All these thoughts begin to run through my head. When I got to where he was standing, he gave the microphone to Carl who gave him a small, and he kneels on one knee. I couldn't believe my eyes.

"Ms. Mariah Marcelo, will you do me the honor of marrying me and becoming my wife?" he asks me.

The church spills over with excitement as I start hearing shouts of "Yes" and "Do it girl" in my ear. I am so shocked, I can't even speak. Instead, tears start to roll down my eyes. I'm overjoyed with happiness. "YES!!!" I scream as we both hug each other tight. I could hear everyone in the church clapping and yelling in the background. They were just as happy as I was. Once we finally let go of each other, Matthew dismissed church.

Matthew and I hugged for what seemed forever. I couldn't believe he asked me to marry him. This was the happiest day of my life. I have to call my mom and tell her the news. I'M GETTING MARRIED!!! I was so excited, I could barely hold myself together. As soon as the church dismissed, people started coming up to me to hug me and tell me congrats, and how excited they were for us. I was taken aback with all the love I was receiving. I could barely get through the floods of people coming at me. I finally reached the doors leading out of the sanctuary when Matthew calls my name and I jump. By this time, the church had cleared out.

"Hey Sweetie. I didn't mean to scare you." Matthew says.

"It's ok. I'm just a little on edge. I'm still in a daze from what just happened." I say, looking at my ring.

"I understand. Wasn't expecting that huh?" Matthew grabs my hands before continuing. "I fell in love with you Mariah Marcelo and you're the one that I want to spend the rest of my life with. I'm sure of that." Matthew says.

As I took in his words, all I could do was cry. "You are the sweetest man that I've ever met and I would love to spend the rest of my life with you." I replied.

"Ok here's the plan. I say we start planning this ASAP. The sooner we can get plans into action, the better. Why don't we go to dinner and celebrate huh?" he says.

"Sounds good to me. I need to go home and change first." I say.

"Ok. I'll meet you at your house, then we can drive together." He tells me.

Jhana came to dinner with us and told me how she was in on the whole thing. I couldn't believe she knew what he was planning. She really did come down to surprise me. There was so much excitement going on in one day and I couldn't believe how Matthew planned everything. Calling Jhana to meet with her and then making sure she was here to see it all.

He's so thoughtful, and he puts his everything in whatever he does. After dinner, we went back to my house so Jhana could get her car and start her drive home. I was sad to see her go but so excited knowing she drove down for this special day. We both hugged and said our goodbyes. After she left and Matthew went home, I had to call my mom and tell her the exciting news.

"Mom this is Mariah."

"Girl, I know who this is. How are you doing?"

"I'm doing good mom, really good. I have something to tell you and dad and it's very important." I say. The suspense was killing me.

"Ok, hold on, let me get your father…
Ok, we're here." She said.

"Ok well, mom, dad. I'm getting married!!!!!" I say screaming.

"OMG!! Really! Is it to that Matthew guy?" My mom asks.

"Yes, it's to the Matthew guy. He proposed today at church, in front of everyone. Jhana came down to see the whole thing!" I was yelling at this point. "She even helped him pick out the ring."

"Wow! I'm so happy Jhana was a part of that. I want to help you plan everything ok? Anything you need, we are here for you." She says. I could hear the happiness in her voice.

"What about you dad? You haven't said much of anything."

In his Korean accent, "I'm really excited. I mean my baby girl is going to get married. You've made

us so proud, Bug. Law school, job right out of college, successful career, and now marrying a handsome, successful preacher. I couldn't ask for a more perfect daughter. Oh yeah. And your sister too." He says laughing.

"Thanks dad. That really means a lot to me. Oh yeah, Matthew wants to fly you guys down here for dinner ASAP. He wants to ask for your blessings dad, and he wants to ask you something too mom but I don't know what." I say to them.

"Oh, he wants to fly us out? I like him already." They replied laughing. "Keep us posted."

"Will do. I Love you guys." I say to them.

"Love you too, Bug." They reply.

At this point, life couldn't get any better. I was at the peak of my career, loving my new life in California, and now I was about to marry the man of my dreams. I mean God has really shined his special light down on me. The only word I can say for that is "Favor". And I'm blessed that God was gracious enough to give me some.

Chapter 7:

The Romance Begins

When Monday morning came, I couldn't wait to get to work and show off my new ring. I'm just hoping that someone notices and asks about it. Matthew and Jhana did a great job picking out the ring. The ring band was rose gold, with small diamonds around the band, and a chocolate diamond in the middle. The way the chocolate diamond complimented my skin, just perfect. Super classy and chic; and I absolutely loved it. Just like our first date, yesterday continued to play over and over in my mind, so surreal. The way he did it in front of the whole church. I know they're all going to want to be a part of the wedding. When he called me down to the altar, I thought I did something wrong or he was about to pray for me. I had no idea that he was going to propose to me. I mean yes, we've been dating for almost a year now, but I still never would've guessed a proposal. When he got down on one knee and popped the question, tears instantly formed in my eyes. I couldn't help myself and I felt so embarrassed crying in front of everyone. Marriage is a very big decision that should not be taken lightly. You are literally making a commitment to share the rest of your life with someone. But there isn't anyone in this world I can think of but him to spend it with.

When I walk into my building, all I can see are eyes. Is there something wrong? Do they know? When I walk into my office, I'm greeted with a bouquet of flowers from Matthew with a card that reads, "To my Flower, have a wonderful day and always keep that shining smile on your face. I love you cakes!" Flower and Cakes are two nicknames that he came up with for me. I'm not exactly sure how those came about, but I like them. Everyone probably wondered what the flowers were for, nothing but two people in love. The card ends with a "P.S. I'll bring you lunch." I can't help but smile... he does so much for me, sometimes it feels unreal.

Sure enough, just as the card said, he brought me lunch from Schlotzsky's. He couldn't stay to eat with me because he had to get back to work for some meetings, but it's the thought that counts. I am always happy to see his smiling face. He told me that his parents were coming to visit us in a few weeks. So, I came up with the thought that both of our parents could come at the same time, so they'd get a chance to meet us and each other. It was hard to believe that in our almost ten months of dating, neither one of us had met each other's parents. That really bothered him because he wanted to talk to my dad and get his blessing before we got married. He's such a gentleman, and I loved that he still wanted my dad's approval. That scored him a few points with my dad too.

Now that the big case with Sam was finally finished, work began to slow down. I took on two small cases but it was nothing compared to the workload with Sam. Sam's case was special to me, from the moment I saw it I knew I had to take it. This man truly had the world against him. We won the case, but it wasn't an easy win. He got a year and a half of being on parole, seeing that he wasn't that bad of a guy to begin with. The judge gave him parole because of the previous charges on his rap sheet. With good behavior, he'd be off within 6-12 months.

Work was under control but my personal life was starting to pick up. Since the proposal, that's the only thing I've been able to focus on. It's almost time for our parents to come into town and I am starting to get really nervous. Not only because it would be our first time meeting each other, but because we have also started the wedding planning as well. I know Matthew's a great and wonderful guy, but I just hope my parents will feel the same way. I always talk about him to my parents, so they have a general idea of what he is like, but it's nothing like the first impression.

We are planning to have the wedding early to mid-May, but we didn't have an exact date just yet, that gave us only 6 months to plan. Things are moving so fast, there was so much stuff going on at church. With the extra rehearsals for the upcoming revival Matthew decided to have, plus the guest artists and preachers we had coming, everything was happening so fast. Not that having a revival is a bad thing, but I just wondered if Matthew really thought all this through. Maybe it wasn't such a good idea to have a revival right now; but then again, you can't question God. He had been telling me for a few months that he was fasting and praying, and God revealed that to him. So, I was behind him 110%.

Before we knew it our parents were here. First to arrive were, The Muleniro's, Matthew's parents. They were coming in tonight, and my parents were scheduled to arrive tomorrow afternoon. Since it was a little late, I decided to cook dinner at my house. They are going to come over after Matthew picks them up from the airport. On the menu was boneless baked chicken, with sausage, vegetables, and a special sauce that I make. I like to add different kinds of fruit to give it a little edgy taste. I love this dish and hope they will like it too.

Before I knew it, Matthew and his parents were knocking at the door and I instantly jump out of my skin. I pull myself together and quickly head to answer the door.

"Hey sweetie." I say to Matthew, kissing him on the cheek as I invite all of them inside my house. "Welcome." I say to his parents.

"Mariah, these are my parents Alessandra and Carlo Muleniro. Mom, Dad, this is my fiancée Mariah." He introduced us.

They both gave me a hug as they walked in. They seemed so warm and welcoming, so that made me feel less nervous. Matthew's mother looked exactly like his older sister Eden. She was average height, with long black curly hair and a beautiful smile. Her teeth were so perfect and white. His father looked exactly like him which let me know Matthew would look good into his older age. He was slightly shorter than Matthew, maybe by an inch or so, with black hair that was cut short. They both had on black jeans, his mom with a nice blouse and his dad with a button up shirt.

"I'm pleased to meet you both. Please come in and make yourself comfortable." I tell them.

"This is a lovely home you have here. Is it just you that lives here?" his mom says to me.

"Yes, just me and my dog Paulo." I chuckle, watching Paulo graze my legs. He knew he was being talked about.

"That's really nice. We've heard a lot about you. When Matthew came to Chicago to visit us a few months ago, all we heard was Mariah this and Mariah that. We couldn't get him to stop talking about you." She says laughing.

"That's nice to hear. It's really nice to finally meet you guys as well. Matthew always tells me stories about you all living in Rome for some time until the both of you decided to move to the states." I replied.

"Yes, all of our children were born there and we moved to Chicago when Matthew turned ten. Carlo was offered a job that we really just couldn't pass up. It was such a great opportunity. God knew exactly what he was doing." She said.

"Doesn't he?" I replied before turning to his dad. "Mr. Muleniro, how did you become a pastor and all, if you don't mind me asking?" I ask his dad.

"Oh no, not at all. The big opportunity was about me becoming a pastor actually. A friend of mine I knew from Chicago called and asked me if I wanted to be his assistant pastor. At the time, I didn't think twice about it and the question was thrown out the window. I couldn't see myself being a pastor, or living in America away from my parents. Even though I was very much involved with the church in Rome, I didn't think I had what it would take to be a pastor of any sort. I also knew Roman and American Christianity were different. Soon after I turned the offer down, God really started working and dealing with my heart. Honestly, I really had no peace until I gave into what I was supposed to do. I really got down to business with the Lord, getting saved and filled with the holy ghost and soon after my friend called back with the same offer and this time I said yes. But my only concern was work and the kids changing schools. But, somehow all that worked out on its own. I already had a job ready for me in Chicago and my kids got accepted into a private school. So, we made the move. My friend passed away and his church is now mine." He told me.

"Wow. That's amazing how God can work everything out for you like that. Long as you're willing to surrender and let him take the wheel." I say back to his father.

"Yes, that is so true. I'm glad that I did surrender and let him take the lead so that I may follow. Nothing but good has come from that move." His dad said.

"And that's all you have to do. Excuse me while I go and check on dinner. Can I get you guys something to drink? Water, soda, juice, anything?" I say.

"Umm, I'll have a glass of water" Replied his mother.

"What kind of juice do you have? His dad asked.

"I have some tea that I made, green tea in the bottle, and apple juice." I replied.

"I'll have some of the tea that you made. Long as it's good." He said jokingly.

"I'm sure that it is. Matthew sure does love it. You want some too Hun? I say to Matthew.

"Yes please." He replies.

I brought them their drinks and let them know dinner was ready. Everything turned out to be great and his parents really enjoyed the meal. After we ate, we talked for a while before they left for their hotel. Matthew stayed and helped me clean up before he left to go home. Sometimes I wish he could just stay with me, but soon enough we'll be together forever. I end my night feeling very accomplished and happy.

Chapter 8:

Let the Planning Begin

Last night was full of good eating and enjoyable conversations. I learned so much about Matthew's family, their time living in Rome, and how he liked growing up in Chicago after being in a totally different continent for so many years. I'm sure that I made a good impression on Matthew's parents too. They left smiling, with a full stomach. Matthew followed behind them, promising to call once he got home. As I was getting settled in for the night, I got a call.

"Hello? Who is this?" I answered. I knew it was Matthew but I played as if I didn't know.

"Hey there, you know it's me Cakes." Matthew replied, catching my playful drift. He made me chuckle. I was glad we could laugh together.

"I had a great time with your parents, they are really nice, I really enjoyed myself. Did they have a good time?" I asked him. I was hoping everyone enjoyed themselves.

"Dinner was amazing and so was the meet and greet. Wouldn't you agree?" He replied. I could tell he was smiling by the tone of his voice.

"It was very nice meeting your parents and everything went a lot smoother than I expected." His tone helped ease the last bit of nerves I had. "But I am still a little nervous for you to meet my parents." I told him.

"I told you my parents would love you and I'm sure all will be well with your parents."

"Yeah, I'm sure you're right. There's no need for nerves. My dad is protective over his girls, but you're an amazing guy. You're just the first real guy I've asked my parents to meet." I felt the nerves setting in again.

"I'll make sure I'm on my best behavior." He said, then started laughing. I could always count on him to remove the seriousness from the moment.

It's Saturday morning and I arose to the alarm blazing in my ear. We have a long day ahead of us, so I needed to get an early start. Looking at the time, I had about an hour to get ready and meet Matthew at the wedding planner's office by ten a.m. We were meeting her to discuss our budget and talk about a few menu items. My parents were arriving at 12:45 pm, so I had to be at the airport to get them. They would come with me downtown where my mom and I had plans to look at wedding dresses. She was so excited; she couldn't even speak on the phone when I told her. Matthew was supposed to meet us downtown also. While we went to the different stores, Matthew and my dad would go and talk about whatever it was Matthew wanted to tell him. Then at 3:00 pm, I was due at the church for a last-minute rehearsal that Carl decided to call as of yesterday. He wanted everyone to go over some songs that we were not only doing for the revival but for service the next day. I really didn't see the point for the extra rehearsal, but then again, he is the choir director. That would last about an hour or so because at 4:30

pm, I needed to stop by my office, meet with my paralegal Claire to pick up some files and some other things for the Tuesday client meeting that we were having, and then off to dinner with the entire family around 7:00 pm or so. I was already getting tired just thinking about what was about to transpire.

I arrived at the wedding planner's office a few minutes early, so I texted Matthew to see if he had arrived. We found her on the internet, and after speaking with her over the phone and seeing her work, I made my decision very quickly. Matthew and I already have some ideas of what we want, so today we are going to establish a budget and tell her what we want so she can come up with some themes. Matthew texted me that he was inside already and I headed in.

"Hello!" She said to both of us as I walked in. "My name is Kristean, welcome to Pristeen Kristean Wedding Planning.

The office was small, like a storefront but the inside design was immaculate and clean. The entire office was decorated in white. Everything from the chairs, desk, curtains and rugs. It reminded me of being younger going to the grocery store with my parents and them warning me not to touch anything. I was curious to know how she kept everything clean. In every corner, there was a pop of color. Pink in one corner, purple in another. With hints of blue and green around as well. It went together so well. She had pictures of brides and wedding venues all throughout. I'd assume people she'd worked with. She also had different hand-written letters thanking her for her help hung around. The aesthetic was bright, yet comforting. I could already tell she paid attention to detail.

"Hello", we both said back. "I'm Mariah and this is Matthew. She reached out to shake out hands. We returned the gesture.

"So glad to meet you in person. Would you like a beverage? Water, wine, or juice?"
I wouldn't dare drink anything other than water with how clumsy I am.

"I'll take water, thank you." I replied. Matthew wanted the same. She gestured us over to some chairs and then left to get the water. When she came back she gave us a checklist to review. This would better help her with planning the wedding.

"Here is my welcome package I give to all my clients during our first meeting. Detailed, you will find a checklist of everything I believe should be completed during the wedding planning. Of course, most of these are suggestions, so there will be some items that will not be completed. That is okay. Every wedding is different. Highlighted are the items that must be completed and the date by when, such as booking a wedding venue and photographer."

The checklist included the theme, budget, wedding party, venue, guest list, photographers, dresses, gift registry, honeymoon, invitations, the cake, and so much more. I was starting to think Matthew's idea of having the wedding in six months wasn't going to happen. He was excited and thought everything could be done within that time frame. He was more involved than I expected him to be, so I figured I'd go along with it. After she gave us the checklist and we talked about everything, she told us what our homework would be for the next meeting.

"Your homework for our next meeting," she paused, "And yes, you will have homework throughout this process." She began to laugh.

"Will be to shop around for venues. Once you find some you like, I will set up meeting times and we will go visit together. In your packet is a list of venues I recommend, but of course you can search on your own. When are you wanting to have your wedding?" She asked.

"We want to get married in six months." Matthew replied. "We were thinking a spring wedding.

"Okay, perfect!", she replied enthusiastically. Her energy made me hopeful. "We will want to find a venue ASAP. Once that is complete, everything else will be easy. How does that sound?"

Matthew and I both looked at each other and shook our heads in agreement. "Sounds like we better get to work." I replied, while letting out a nervous chuckle.

"Don't worry. I am here to help with everything. Don't hesitate to call or reach out with any questions. You'll have the wedding of your dreams. Don't forget to fill out the paperwork and we'll review at our next meeting."

"Okay, great. That sounds perfect." Matthew replied as we all stood and headed for the door.

"Thank you Kristean, talk to you soon!" I said, walking out the door.

It was only about 2:30 pm in the afternoon and I felt so tired. I was already beginning to get worn out and the day wasn't even halfway over. Once our meeting with the wedding planner was over, I rushed to the airport to get my parents. Of course, there was traffic as I was heading there, but they didn't have to wait too long. As soon as I picked them up, we headed downtown to meet Matthew. Not soon after we get downtown, it was nearly time to head to the church for rehearsal. The time was flying by. I was still with my mom when I looked at the clock and realized we needed to leave. I was having such a good time talking with her, I didn't want it to end. And I sure didn't want to go to the rehearsal, but it was too late to bail or cancel now. UGH! I wasn't prepared for this. My mom decided that she'd come with me to the rehearsal instead of being dropped off at the hotel she and my dad were staying at. It would give me a chance to introduce her to everyone and she can see me in action after so many years. I would also get to spend some extra time with her. My dad was having such a great time with Matthew, he decided to stay with him.

We arrived at the church at about ten minutes past three, I knew I was going to hear from Carl about being late, but at this point, I didn't care. I've been running around all day and I am exhausted. I was ready to get there, go over the songs, and get out, still having so much more stuff to do afterwards.

When everyone saw my mom, all I heard was how beautiful she is and how much I look just like her. They were all so excited to meet the, "woman that gave birth to this bunch of talent", they said. That made her feel special, as she smiled from ear to ear, I could tell she was proud of me.

Rehearsal lasted about an hour and a half, making me late to my next appointment with Claire. I had to stop by my office to meet with my paralegal Claire, to discuss some things and pick up some files for a Tuesday client meeting. She let me know that she was going to be late too, so we met up at five o'clock pm instead of four-thirty. I guess it all worked out alright. Even though I was exhausted, my mom was having a great time which made me happy. She was able to see the different sites as we drove past them and experienced some of the great food and shopping LA had to offer. She saw the church, my office, and soon she would be able to see my house. This was her first time in L.A., and I knew that she wouldn't forget it. I wanted my mom and dad to have the best time they possibly could. Although, I was sure they would be visiting more often now.

After exchanging words with Claire and figuring out what was going to happen on Tuesday, it was now six-thirty. By this time, Matthew had gone and picked up his parents and they were just driving around. We agreed to have dinner at seven-thirty at Maestro's Grill which was a small chain restaurant in Downtown, LA. They had some of the best burgers, salads, and fried fish in town. My dad is pescatarian so we had to always find a place we could all enjoy. He always had to be the odd ball. When he called me, I told him that I was tired and I was going to go home and lay down for a while before dinner. He said that they'd meet my mom and I there so I could relax a little.

When I got home, I went straight to my bed and laid down. Matthew, my dad, and his parents arrived shortly after. Matthew joined me upstairs and we laid there talking about the day we just had, while our parents were downstairs acquainting themselves. Since my dad had already met Matthew's parents, it was mainly my mom being filled in. It seemed like as soon as I laid down, it was time to get up. It was already seven-fifteen which meant it was time to leave my house to go to the restaurant. I already knew what I was going to order before we even got there.

Dinner ended up going very well. Matthew's parents and I ordered a cheeseburger with fries. My mom and dad ordered Fish and Chips, and Matthew some weird looking dish that he apparently said was good. We all shared great conversations, sharing stories of church and family life. I really got to see a different side of Matthew, being around his parents. He's always laid back but he was even more relaxed around his parents. It was evident how much he loves and cares for his parents. He treated his mother well and gave his father a type of respect as if he looked up to him. As I sat here and reflected on the past few months, I feel even more assured I am in good hands being with him. I looked over at him and gave a smile, and he smiled back as well. Today was an exciting and eventful day, but I was so ready to go home and crawl in the bed. I am so tired, and we have church in the morning, which means another busy day ahead. A nice hot bath was calling my name. We left the restaurant, headed back to my house, and everyone went to their respective places of rest. I was excited to see them all again for church the next morning.

Chapter 9:

Nostalgia

I was up early for church but I was still so tired. My phone rang, and to my surprise it was Matthew.

"Good morning beautiful".

"Good morning". I said, trying not to sound too grouchy.

"I just wanted to let you know that I love you, and can't wait to see you in a few hours".

His words made me blush, it was exactly what I needed to hear to get my day going. I was excited to hear his voice, which gave me an extra pep in my step. My parents were especially excited to go to church this morning as well. They couldn't wait to hear me play and Matthew preach. I really couldn't believe how long it had been since I last saw them and even longer since I played for them. Growing up, church on Sundays was a part of our normal routine, where I played for the praise team. But, between school, graduation, and preparing for the Bar exam, I didn't have much time to go visit my home church. I was blessed that they were here to see me now, and that they could see that I have another wonderful church to play at. Church, here I come.

After service, I made my usual rounds and talked to some of the saints. Deacon Jones and Mother Massy greeted me before I met with my parents.

"Sister Mariah, where did you learn to play that organ like that?" Mother Massy asked me.

"Well mother, I can't take any of the credit, it all comes from God. And that's who I thank every day for it." I reply.

"Well keep on baby girl, because I love to hear you play every Sunday. Yes, yes indeed." She said to me, smiling and walking away.

"Thank you Mother Massy, it's a pleasure to play for you all." I replied. She was my favorite.

"Mariah, it's so good to hear you play Sunday after Sunday. It never gets old and you seem to get better and better." Deacon Jones said to me.

"Thank you, Deacon. Gotta stay on top of it, so I can continue making a joyful noise."

"Sweet, sweet music to my ears. We're so blessed to have you here, and now you'll be here even longer, First Lady. Congrats again on the engagement." He said.

I was smiling ear to ear now. That was the first time anyone mentioned me being Matthew's first lady. I think it fit me, but also made me nervous having to uphold such a title.

"Thank you so much deacon. It really is a privilege to play for you all. And even more of a privilege to be you all's first lady soon. Keep me in your prayers. I want to make everyone proud." I replied to him.

"Make God proud and you'll make us proud." He said as he walked away.

From the moment I walked into the church, everyone here took me in. They never treated me like a visitor. That was one thing that stood out to me while making my decision to become a member. They were so welcoming, and people need that. I was excited to be a part of something so much bigger than myself. Matthew set such a great foundation and I hope that I will be able to keep that up. I finally caught up with my parents after talking to everyone.

"Wow, Mariah! I almost forgot how good you play. It's been so long since I've heard you Bug. I've missed you and that beautiful playing." My dad said to me.

"Thanks dad, that means a lot. Everyone here loves my playing, I must admit, I love it here also." I said to him. "I've missed you both too."

"I loved it when you played classical music at your recitals. You always made me proud, both of my girls. I couldn't ask for any better daughters." He said to me.

"Thanks dad. I love you so much! You raised us right and in the Lord. That's why we are the way we are today." I replied back.

Some of the members needed to speak with Matthew after service, so we all waited for him in the foyer. I couldn't help but start wondering how things would be once we get married. Would they want to speak with me also? How would my role change to assist him and the church? Would it be hard for everyone to adjust? How would our lives change? He does such a great job at handling everything and I'm sure everyone is used to coming to him for help. I want to be a part of everything and help wherever I can. I wasn't exactly sure how my new role as first lady would be or even what he'd want me to do differently. At the same time, I was so excited to dive into everything, but I want to do the best job I can. I'll talk to him about it later. We have been doing our best at having those hard conversations to avoid as much conflict as we could. So, I felt this was right up that alley.

Matthew finally came out of the office so we could go and eat. Something we both loved to do.

Our parents were tired after dinner, so they decided to head to their hotels for an early night. Matthew and I had some appointments tomorrow for the wedding, so we decided to take the day off and spend it with each other, which I was really looking forward to. We talked for a while in the parking lot before parting our separate ways home.

I was really enjoying the time with my parents. It had been so long since I'd seen them. I missed them so much and I wanted to enjoy all the time I could with them. I was so happy they liked Matthew. Their approval meant a lot to me, and it turned out, I had nothing to be worried about. Matthew and my dad had a great talk and he approved of him asking for my hand in marriage and my mom loved talking with Matthew's mom. They even swapped numbers so they could exchange ideas about the wedding and whatever else they had in mind. Our parents meeting each other couldn't have gone any better. And that was all I could ask for. I knew our time together was coming to an end, but I didn't want to think about that. I knew they'd be back soon for the wedding. It was a bittersweet ending to a great and successful trip.

Chapter 10:

Spiraling

It is crazy to think we were only two months from the wedding. The wedding was beginning to come along so well, as we have gotten most of the hard stuff out of the way. The date was set, April 7th. We had the church picked out, our church of course. We had a place for the reception and it wasn't far away from the church which was perfect. I saw plenty of bridesmaids dresses I liked and finally decided to go with these yellow strapless ones. Each dress would be a slight variation of the maid of honor's dress, which I thought was cool and unique. Matthew had also picked out the tuxedos and bow ties for the men, traditional tuxedos with yellow bow ties. We decided that our wedding color and theme would be around yellow, for the spring. We had yellow decorations all over; napkins, table cloths and bows for the chairs, flowers inside clear vases with yellow glitter around them. We even decided to give away gift bags with various yellow things inside for the guests. Now all that was left was to get everything fitted and ordered. Our wedding was now about two months away, our early start on planning helped us to be able to set the date a little earlier. That also gave us a little breathing room because we knew we had extra time to spare.

This weekend the bridesmaids and I were going to do a fitting for their dresses. My maid of honor is my sister Jhana. The bridesmaids are Krystal, Claire, Matthew's sister Eden, and a friend of mine from college Samantha. Matthew's groomsmen were his brother Jordan who was his Best Man, Daniel, James from his job, Carl the choir director, and Case, his friend from back home. There were five people on each side. It was beginning to be a big wedding, but I wouldn't let it get too big. We asked his dad to officiate the wedding. He was so excited that we chose him for this special day. He said he'd be honored to marry us. It was still hard to believe all of this was happening. The wedding planning was going great so far, and our wedding planner really knew what she was doing. Every idea we gave her, she took and made it bigger and better. I was getting the wedding of my dreams and Matthew was super happy as well.

Like every couple getting married, you always start with a budget and you try hard not to go outside of it, but like most people, I did. I bought a few extra things that we probably really didn't need but I wanted it. It was my big day and I wanted to have everything I possibly could. I was hoping Matthew wouldn't find out, but unfortunately, he did. We agreed to not do the special made napkins that I wanted.

"Sweetie, I want you to have everything you want, but we've already ordered decorated napkins and just think, people will be wiping their faces with them. Not worrying about what's on them. Right?" Matthew said to me.

I just took that and ran with it. There wasn't much I could really say after he said that? He spoke, and I had to listen. I knew I was getting beside myself but he didn't want to spend more money than we needed too, and he was right. I loved that he was so gentle with me, he didn't raise his voice or yell. He just simply told me I was doing more than I needed and there was no point in the extra napkins. I know I could follow a man like that.

As the wedding date gets closer, the pressure is really starting to build up. Things were coming up that Matthew and I never really worried about but now they were becoming more and more relevant. On top of the wedding, I became more and more part of the church staff. Meaning working with children, choir, and anywhere else I was needed. I found myself at the church almost three, sometimes four days a week with Matthew. I didn't mind being there, but everything was starting to spiral out of control; I was beginning to lose it. Even work started to pick up, which was all I needed. For some reason, every case that someone didn't want, they recommended the client to me. And with my reputation being in tack, of course they choose me to represent them. With me being who I am, I always said yes. I was juggling two cases and I knew I wasn't giving either one of them the full attention they needed. I was doing enough, but I knew I could do more if I had the time. It was already too late to give them away and I had Claire doing most of the work, which again I wasn't too happy about.

I tried to figure out which activity to cut out or at least slow down on, so I could have at least one day to recuperate. The wedding was right around the corner, so no halting on that. I needed my job, so I had to keep working. That only left church, which was a commitment that I didn't really want to cut down on either. I decided instead of being at the church three to four days a week, it went down to only two days a week. For the first time since I moved to California, I was busy every day of the week; I didn't know what to do with myself.

Soon Matthew began to see me a little more tired than usual. By the time I got home, it was around eleven at night, then winding down from the day's work, I eventually fell asleep between twelve-thirty and one in the morning, to wake at six forty-five and do it all over again. Matthew had approached me Thursday after rehearsal very concerned.

"Cakes, what's the matter? You haven't been yourself these past two weeks?" he said to me.

"I'm just tired that's all. There's a lot of stuff going on right now, as you can tell." I replied.

"Well, what else do you have going on besides the wedding?"

"You know I told you about those two cases I took on. Plus, the work here at the church I'm doing."

"Well, you look really tired and I don't like that. You're doing way too much right now. You're going to work yourself sick." He said to me sternly.

"Matthew, I know that, but there isn't much that I can do about it right now. I've already cut down on some things."

"Yes, you can. I can take over the Wednesday work here at the church and the choir can do without you for a few weeks. They managed it before, you can go home on those days and get some sleep."

"Ok, but what about Sunday worship and stuff?"

"Mariah, I will tell Carl that you won't be at rehearsals for a while. I mean of course you can still play during church, I wouldn't tell you to stop that, just maybe not the new songs. He will just have to understand that there's a lot going on right now. You look exhausted every day that I see you. Emilio can handle the keyboard and music for a few weeks. You can go back after everything calms down a little. That's what's happening and there's nothing more that will be said. Ok?"

"Yea, ok." I replied.

After he said that, I wasn't really sure what to say to him but ok. After a little talk and reassurance, he kissed me goodnight and I headed home, bound for the bed. Not working those extra days at the church would make a big difference. I was actually happy he took over Wednesdays at the church. It would really give me some breathing room and time to rest.

Friday morning, I decided to go to work a little later than usual. I was able to sleep in and it made the world's difference. I got to work around 10:30 a.m. to find flowers on my desk from Matthew. It had a card that said, "Cakes, I know you've been working a lot and juggling everything on your plate, but I'm here to help you. All you have to do is say so. Ok? I love you and I'll see you at lunch! Love Matthew." After reading that I could do nothing but smile. He always makes me feel better, no matter what the situation is. From that moment I knew I was going to have a good day.

Matthew came around one forty-five. to bring me lunch from Carl's Bistro. They sell salads and sandwiches of all sorts; he brought me my favorite Caesar salad with extra shredded chicken and cheese. We sat in my office eating and talking about almost everything. He didn't have to go back to work, so he stayed with me for a while. He was a big help to me and Claire since we had so much to do in such little time. He helped put away some files and paperwork I had laying around and organized the files in my cabinet. My office was so messy with all the cases I've been handling. We were preparing for court for one of the cases, and the second case's court dates were right around the corner. Everything was falling in line, after that second case, the wedding would be about two and a half weeks away. So, I guess everything worked out for the good.

I left the office around nine-thirty, a little earlier than I expected but with Matthew there to help us, we accomplished a lot. After we left the office, Matthew and I went to his house to relax before I departed home. We were getting some things in order for our meeting tomorrow with the wedding planner. Now with the venue for the wedding and the reception booked, photographers hired, music and entertainment booked, both bridesmaids and wedding dresses purchased, and important documents ordered and out the way, we could start focusing on some other things. Invitations had also been sent out and people started to RSVP. That helped us to begin the seating arrangements for the reception. Tomorrow we were going to finalize the menu and get them printed. I wanted to have at least five to six people seated at each table. The wedding cake has also been ordered.

We have a little less than two months to go and I thought we were doing pretty well for ourselves. The biggest thing that needed to be finalized was making our final list from all the RSVP's. Everything else was pretty much set in stone. I had a few more fittings for my wedding dress and that special day would be here in no time.

Chapter 11:

The Rehearsal

Now about a week away from the wedding, the next thing on our agenda was the rehearsal dinner. I looked down at my phone, realizing I had received a text from Jhana saying she was on her way to the church for the rehearsal dinner. In attendance would also be my parents, two aunts and uncles, grandparents from both sides, and the wedding party. The rehearsal dinner slowly seemed to be turning into a family reunion rather than a rehearsal dinner. I pray this dinner doesn't backfire. The purpose was to ensure everything ran smoothly without any hiccups, work out the logistics, and answer questions. This would be our day and I wanted it to stay like that.

Instantly I started shaking, my nerves began to rise, and I felt my heart beating fast. My palms were wet, but the webs of my fingers were dry. Maybe it finally hit me that I'm getting married in a few days. My life is about to change forever, but I'm not quite sure how to feel. I went downstairs to finish getting ready before heading to the church myself. It was time to get the day started. I took a moment to breathe, this was the change I had been waiting for.

When I arrived at the church, everyone was conjugating outside, I assumed waiting for me.

"Why is everyone outside?" I asked Jhana. I felt as though the car ride helped calm me down, but seeing everyone outside suddenly made me anxious again.

"Matthew, his dad, and the wedding planner wanted to sort out some stuff before everyone went in. They're waiting for you inside. We just decided to stay out here and talk, not to disturb them." Jhana replied, winking at me. She was really turning out to be the best Maid of Honor ever.

I walked inside the church and was greeted by Matthew, the wedding coordinator and his dad.

"She's here!", Kristean yelled. Hello Bride and hello again Groom!" Kristean said to Matthew and I as I walked into the church. One thing I loved about Kristean was her fun energetic personality. Her presence always filled a room.

"Hello Kristean." We both replied as I gave her a hug and Matthew shook her hand again.

"Are we ready to get this show on the road? I can't wait to share this day with you both!" She was almost jumping up and down at this point.

"Yeah, we guess so." Matthew replied, looking at me confused. I chuckled and we walked into the church. I realized early on, Kristean had no issues being herself. She was dorky, but it worked for her. She loved her work and was great at it. She easily put her all in everything she did.

The rest of our bridal party began to make their way in, as I started introducing Kristean to everyone. She immediately got to work arranging everyone and lining them up with their respective partners. Luckily, she was on top of everything because I would have forgotten my head if it wasn't attached to my neck at this very moment. It was all so overwhelming. She made sure all the bridal party knew their places and where to stand at which times. She ensured the music would be played correctly and which songs were to be played at which moments. She also made sure Matthew and I didn't have to tell anyone anything, I mean she was really on top of everything. The only thing that was missing were the wedding decorations.

The rehearsal lasted about an hour or so, which was perfect because I realized I didn't eat before coming here. I guess it was my nerves and now that I calmed down for good, I was hungry. Everyone made their way to the back of the church where the kitchen was to have dinner as a family. The food was catered by none other than our own Deacon Brown, who was also catering our wedding. He cooked for almost every occasion the church had, so it was an easy decision to have him cater the wedding as well. As a wedding gift, he volunteered to cater the rehearsal dinner which was totally unexpected. You could instantly smell all the southern aromas in the foyer. He cooked traditional soul food, greens, cabbage, cornbread, ham, macaroni and cheese, turkey and dressing, and peach cobbler for dessert. It felt like Sunday dinner at grandma's house, everyone sitting around the dinner table sharing stories from the week, unwinding not having a care in the world. And that's how we all ate. Sitting around the table, reminiscing about old times instantaneously creating new ones.

I told some of my other family members to meet at the church after the rehearsal for the dinner so everyone could be together. It had been so long since I saw all my family and I wanted to spend as much time together during these few days as I could. Everyone enjoyed the food and I made my rounds catching up with all my aunts, uncles, and cousins. Some of Matthew's family and friends met us for the dinner and I was able to meet them as well. My sister insisted on us making a toast for the upcoming days. I wasn't one to give speeches or talk, despite me being a lawyer, if I didn't have to. I felt my nerves rushing up again. During that moment, I wanted to crawl into my grandmothers' arms and hide from the world. All eyes were on Matthew and me.

"I just want to thank everyone for the great rehearsal today. Matthew and I can't wait to share the big day with you all. We appreciate your support and love throughout this whole process. And most of all, for traveling various distances to be here with us. A special thank you to Kristean for being such a great wedding coordinator." Everyone started clapping for her. She decided to stay and eat with us, after originally planning to leave after the rehearsal. "She has been amazing during this process and I can't wait for you all to see the final product she's put together. The next few days will be fun filled and busy, so I encourage you all to enjoy it. Myself included. Love you all!"

Matthew agreed with what I said and didn't feel the need to add anything else. After the toast, we continued eating and chatting before starting to clean up. The night had grown long and it was time to relax. Finally, the dinner was over, and I could take everyone to their respective hotels. I'd say the dinner was a success.

My sister was staying the night with me to catch up on some much-needed sister time.

"Girl, I feel like it's been so long! Tell me everything that's going on." Jhana said, almost yelling from excitement.

"Well, what do you want to know?" I asked laughing, I wasn't even sure where to begin.

"How has everything been so far with Matthew? You're getting married soon!" She was now yelling at this point. Jhana had no way of hiding her excitement.

"It's going great really. I have no complaints." I replied. By the look on her face, I could tell I wasn't giving her the details she wanted.

"Vague much?" She said laughing. "I just mean, I've never seen you this happy. Well, not that you weren't happy before, but you're always smiling and talking about what you and Matthew are about to go and do. Every Facebook status is, "Dinner with Matthew, talking with Matthew, Wedding's in two weeks! Marrying the man of my dreams…""

"Ok, ok. I get it. Matthew's always the topic of discussion." I said laughing. "But when you fall in love with someone. Like really fall in love with them, you can't help but to always talk about them. They're always on your mind and you start to think about your future together. Really, since we started to plan this wedding, I haven't been able to focus 100% on my work. Lately, all I find myself thinking about is the wedding, and what we have to do next, and what's coming up. Even though I'm having a ball, I'm also being a little stressed planning this wedding, I will be glad when it's over." I interrupted her. "I'm ready to just be in the moment with him and start our lives together." I continued.

"Wow. The feeling of love, it just sounds so… so amazing. I think I have a little more work to do with my boyfriend. So, what are you guys doing for your honeymoon?" she asked, smiling.

"Well honestly, I don't know. Matthew said that he wanted to plan all that, so I said sure why not. It was one less thing for me to do and have to worry about. All I know is that we're flying somewhere, but I don't know where. Maybe it'll be to Rome. I'd love to go there."

"Wow. That would be cool. Isn't that where he's from?"

"Yes, basically all his family lives there besides his parents, brother and sister."

"I'd love to go there too. It looks so pretty, and there's so much history."

"I know, he told me about some of the history and it's just amazing. I told him I wanted to go there soon. So, we'll see what happens. But wherever we go, I know it'll be nice because he's really romantic."

"Awwww, that's really sweet. Shoot. Maybe I should marry a pastor." She said laughing.

"Hey, if God leads you to do that, then there's nothing that you can do about it."

"Yeah, that is true also."

"Of course it is." I replied laughing.

"Okay miss smarty pants. I really miss our sisterly bonding time. I mean, I haven't really, really seen you since you left for college. There were always breaks and things like that, but those were always so short. Especially after being together all of our lives. It's kind of sad when your other half leaves, and the sad part about it is that we live two hours away from each other and we haven't really seen each other in like three years. Just quick trips here and there. Totally unacceptable." Jhana said.

"Yeah, that is so true, just talking over the phone mainly. Seems like we've grown apart a little bit and I don't like that. We have to promise that we'll see each other more, no matter what. Like once a week or something, or even a few times a month will do."

"I promise that. I love you little sis."

"I love you too sis."

We ended our conversation and fell asleep, resting up for spa day tomorrow with the girls.

Chapter 12:

Tick... Tock...

The next day, Jhana and I woke up at about nine-thirty to prepare for the big day we had ahead of us. We were meeting the bridal party, and Matthew and I's mothers at the spa for a long day of pampering. I couldn't wait, I hadn't had a massage in forever, and I had some tension in my back that needed to be relieved. We didn't know how long the spa would take us, so the whole day was dedicated to us being pampered. Of all the extra activities we had planned, I was looking forward to this day the most. Not just because it was a spa day, but this would be a really good time to bond with some of my closest friends. Even though I see them almost every day, it would be nice to talk about something other than work or what was happening next week at church. When we all got to the Spa, the staff greeted us with wine to celebrate me getting married in a few days.

We spent the day getting facials, manicures and pedicures, and indulging in some much-needed girl talk. I figured everyone heard enough about my relationship, so it was nice to hear about the other girls dating lives. It was awesome having our mothers there as well. They gave us some good advice about dating and marriage.

"What advice would you give us about dating and marriage?" I asked the mothers.

"Well, I would say to put God first in your marriage. And in your life. You'd be amazed at how many problems we cause for ourselves by always trying to do it our own way." Matthew's mom replied.

"I learned that the hard way." My mom chimed in, as everyone began to laugh.

My mom continued.

"Your dad and I went through a trying time when he was still in the navy. It was right before you were born. It was so bad, we considered divorce. We were both tired of fighting each other and never tackled the problem we had. We never considered what we would lose if we got a divorce, or even how that would affect the kids."

"How did you make it through? What was the turning point?" My sister asked.

We were all so curious to know how they made it through. I was especially curious because I knew Matthew and I would probably face some hard times during our marriage.

"Honestly, I realized how much I loved your father and how different my life would be without him. Neither of us choose to take the low road and apologize for our parts in the hurt. So, I decided to do just that. I apologized for my part and let him know that I didn't want the marriage to end. I was willing to do whatever I needed in order to make things work. And thankfully he agreed. We started praying and reading our word together every day and putting God first in our marriage and left our egos at the door. Things got so much better and we never looked back. We realized it was us against the issue, not against each other."

We were all so intrigued by her story, the room fell silent. At that moment, I realized that marriage was more than just me and him. It was truly me, him, and God.

Matthew and I spent so much time discussing how we wanted our marriage to look and the type of relationship we wanted. We both had so many plans and ideas, but I knew how important it would be for us to remember not only why we got married, but how to keep our relationship on the up and up. My mom may not have realized it, but her advice was some of the best advice I received. We continued talking about relationships, marriage, and finding a balance. Matthew's mom gave us advice about being married in ministry and some of the sacrifices she made so they could have the life they live now. All of us younger ladies ate each of their words up. I hope the others learned something from them today.

I had such a good time with the girls at the spa and the time went by so fast. They say time flies when you're having fun, and that day it proved to be true. We left around five o'clock to head to dinner with the groomsmen and Matthew. We decided to go to Red Lobster, since none of us had been there in a while. I hadn't spoken to Matthew all day, which was weird considering we talk every day multiple times a day. I couldn't wait to get there to see him.

"Hey cakes, I missed you today." He said as he greeted me with a kiss and a hug at Red Lobster.

"I know, I missed you too. The girls told me it was a day for pampering and that we weren't allowed to talk to any guys. Jhana didn't even let Krystal call Daniel and you know that's a surprise because they eat, live, and breathe through each other." I said as I kissed him and began to laugh. "She really wanted us to relax and enjoy each other's company."

"Ha, well I see. You guys look like you accomplished a lot. What did you get done?" he asked.

"Well, we got manicures and pedicures, massages, facials, sat in the steam room for like half an hour, and just talked and had a good time. How was your day?" I replied.

"Sounds like you had a really good day. My day was good also, I just hung out with the guys and had some "guy time". He said laughing. "What's in store for tomorrow?" he asked.

"All of us including your mom and mine will be going to get our hair done. And then my mom and Jhana are staying with me for the night to prepare for Saturday. I'm so happy everything is finally done and we can get this show on the road." I replied back.

"Yes, I agree with you all the way. I can't wait, just two more days."

"Oh and thanks for paying for our day. That was really sweet of you to do." I said smiling.

"Oh, you're welcome. Daniel told me that all the ladies were going to the spa for the day and I didn't know who was paying for it since you didn't say anything to me about it. So, I went there earlier and gave them my credit card number and told them to charge whatever you guys got done to my tab." He said.

"Well, I really appreciate that." I said.

"You are most welcome, I love you, I'd do anything for you." He told me.

Right then, I just melted all over again. This reminded me exactly why I was marrying this man standing in front of me.

"I love you too Matthew." I said back to him.

After dinner, we all departed our separate ways saying goodbye. Jhana and I went back to my house to relax and wind down from the day's actions. Again, we had a long talk that night about the wedding Saturday and how I was feeling before going to bed. I couldn't even express to her how excited I was. I was at such a loss for words. Saturday would be the happiest day of life. I was going to marry the man that I love and be with him forever.

After we talked a little, we headed to bed for the night. Tomorrow will be another busy day, but not as exciting since we were just going to get our hair done and that would probably take all day. There was so much going on and so much that still needed to be done. The wedding was now a day away and I had so much on my mind I could hardly sleep. Plus, all our families were in town, so I wanted to spend as much time with them as I could. It was all a little overwhelming, but I was glad things calmed down a lot from a few months ago when my head was spinning. We were now in the home stretch.

It took me about two hours to go to bed that night. When Jhana and I finally stopped talking, it was already about midnight, and when I went to sleep, it was almost two-thirty in the morning. I knew I was going to pay for it because I had to get up early in the morning. Since it was about ten of us getting our hair done by the two stylists, on the same day, around the same time, it was going to be a very long day.

Jhana and I arrived first at Dare to Wear Your Hair, also known as just Dare and my mom arrived shortly after. Since I was the only one getting my hair colored, Missy decided to do my hair first out of us two. The others hadn't arrived, and mine would probably take the longest. I was getting highlights, bangs, and just a flat iron because tomorrow, she'd come to my house and style my hair for the wedding. I picked the hair style I wanted months ago while I planned everything

else. Jhana and my mom decided to get about 4 inches cut off their hair, and all the bridesmaids were getting sleek ponytails. My sister liked to keep her hair shorter because it was easier to maintain and my mom liked hers longer.

It was about ten-thirty and the rest of the clan arrived for their hair appointments. They were late, as I already knew they would be. My thought was the sooner I got there, the sooner I could leave. I realized that I hadn't talked to Matthew since last night, which wasn't very long ago, but I really wanted to hear his voice. While I sat under the dryer, I texted him. Even though I couldn't really hear his voice, I could still talk to him.

Mariah: Hey sweetie! Are you awake?

Matthew: Hey cakes. Yes I am. Where are you?

Mariah: @ Dare. I miss you.

Matthew: I miss you 2. Will I be able to see you at least once 2day?

Mariah: Umm, I'm not sure how long this will take. Jhana and I got here on time, so we were able to get in 1st. So we should be done here pretty soon but I wasn't sure if I was going to leave right after I'm done.

Matthew: Oh ok. I'm headed over to the barber shop now. I got to get ready for the big day 2mro too.

Mariah: Yes, I suppose u do. ☺ Sometimes it's still hard to believe that we're tying the knot. I'm glad you're the man I'm marrying.

Matthew: I couldn't see myself with any1 else. You're everything and more than a man could ask for.

Mariah: I feel the same way.

Matthew: What other plans do you have today?

Mariah: Honestly, probably just eat and get ready for tomorrow. I'm sure I'll be here for a while. What about you?

Matthew: Just get ready for tomorrow.

I literally laughed out loud. By this time, I could sense Jhana's eyes staring me down while she sat a few dryers away from me. We followed the typical rules of the bride and groom not seeing each other before the wedding, but she read somewhere talking to each other is bad luck too. Jhana had always been a little superstitious and I knew she wouldn't let it go. I'd sneak and talk to him later.

Mariah: I hate to go, but Jhana is staring me down to put my phone away...

Matthew: It's okay LOL. I'll let you go, and I'll talk to you a little later.

Mariah: Yes. I love you.

Matthew: I love you too!

And that ended our conversation.

After Jhana reminded me about her superstitions about talking to the groom before the wedding, it was time for me to wash the color out of my hair. She really wanted all of us to bond and enjoy each other's company anyway, as the men were doing as well. She didn't realize how much I missed Matthew these last few days. We'd only seen each other like twice and I hardly spoke to him. I knew she meant well, but I missed my man. I tried not to think about it too much, since we'd be reunited tomorrow. And I was really excited for this new look I was going to have.

As it turned out, I absolutely loved the bangs and highlights. I couldn't wait for Matthew to see what it looked like. After finishing my hair and waiting for all the others to finish, it was already about six-thirty. It would just be me and the girls for the rest of the night till it was time to go and turn in for the BIG day we all had ahead of us. I could hardly wait!

When everyone's hair was finished, we went out for my Bachelorette Party. It wasn't the typical "bachelorette party" with stripers and drinking because that wasn't my scene. Of course, some of my friends tried to plan one of those parties but I had to stop that before they proceeded. Instead, we all enjoyed a nice dinner at one of my favorite restaurants, then headed back over to my house for a few hours of girl talk, some glasses of wine and gifts. That was the bachelorette party that I wanted, and I had a wonderful time.

Soon enough, everyone left for their destinations to get a good night's rest for tomorrow. My mom and both my grandmothers stayed the night at my house to help me prepare tomorrow. It would beat them waking up super early to get to my house when they could already be there. The wedding would start promptly at two-thirty and I wanted everything to start on time, so the more help I had, the better.

It wasn't hard for my mom, sister, and grandmothers to fall asleep. But I on the other hand couldn't sleep to save my life. I just found myself laying in the bed thinking about absolutely nothing except tomorrow. I knew I would be tired, but I was sure with all the excitement and everything that was going on, I would stay awake somehow. I wanted to get at least some sleep before my big day. I couldn't imagine dozing off during something so special because I was tired. I put some Jazz music on to help ease my mind, which usually helped. And with that I drifted off into sleep.

Chapter 13:

The Big Day

The morning finally came. After getting only about four and half hours of sleep last night, I'm already beat. That all goes away when my sister comes into my room and yells, "IT'S THE BIG DAY!! YAY!!! GET UP GIRL!!". That was all the waking up that I needed.

After being startled by my sister, I laid in the bed a little while longer after she left. I wasn't sure how to feel, but my emotions were everywhere. I was tired, happy, and anxious. But most of all, I couldn't stop thinking about Matthew. I hadn't seen or talked to him much the last few days with everything going on. It was probably the longest we've gone without talking to each other. I wondered if he got as much sleep as I did. I wondered if he was as nervous as I was. I wondered if he missed me as much as I missed him. I decided to text him before diving into the craziness of the day.

Mariah: Good morning my love

Matthew: Good morning! This is wild

Immediately my heart dropped. I assumed something bad happened.

Mariah: ...what?

Matthew: You're really going to be my wife and I'm really going to be your husband.

Mariah: This is it. No take backsies. Forever.

Matthew: I wouldn't take it back for anything else.

Mariah: Me either baby, I can't wait to spend forever with you.

After sending that last text, I sat up in the bed mentally preparing myself for the day. Thoughts began to flood my head, as the adrenaline began to pick up. From hair, make-up, packing my bag for the church, and making sure nothing was left behind, I began to feel overwhelmed. I took a deep breath before heading downstairs to get everything started.

"GOOD MORNING!" Everyone shouted as I walked down the stairs.

"Good morning", I replied back. Startled by how awake everyone was. I was still trying to figure life out at that point.

"Here's a plate. We have to make sure you eat something before the ceremony. Nobody wants a hungry bride." My sister immediately handed me a plate before I had a chance to sit down. I could feel my stomach starting to turn with all the smells from the food.

"Thanks, but I'm not really hungry right now." I couldn't fathom the thought of food at that moment. My nerves were getting the best of me. I felt like I was shaking in my own skin. I could hardly wait to walk down the aisle and marry the man of my dreams.

"Nope. Not taking no for an answer. Here, eat something, fruit, anything. Take a deep breath. Everything is going to be perfect." Jhana had the biggest smile on her face, and it was so reassuring. It made me believe everything was going to be okay, so I started eating.

My mom made sure the hair stylist and makeup artist came to the house to do our hair and makeup. It was so much more convenient since everyone was there. I was second to go and my sister would go after me so we could head to the church. I would finish getting ready there. The entire house was chaotic all morning. From clothes everywhere, dishes all over the counters, people yelling over who's shirt belonged to whom: it was so loud I couldn't hear myself think. I felt like screaming at all of them to just be quiet. I wanted to save all my energy for the ceremony and reception. So instead, I went to my room for a few minutes to regroup before heading to the church to get dressed. I took a few more deep breaths before me, my sister, mom and grandmothers all left the house. They would help me finish getting dressed there. Claire stayed behind, earning the friend of the year award making sure I had everything ready for my trip. I had already packed everything, but she told me she'd bring my bags to the hotel after the reception. She also grabbed our marriage license and made sure everyone else at my house was okay.

When I arrive at the church, I see all my friends and family outside the church and in the foyer. Everyone looked so beautiful all dolled up. I loved seeing all their loving faces. It had been so long since I'd seen some of them. I go into Matthew's office where my dress is and have some alone time before the wedding starts. I say a little prayer to myself,

> "Lord, I ask that you guide Matthew and I through this long journey that we are about to begin. I know that he is the man that you have saved and given to me. I ask that you give me the wisdom and knowledge to know what is best for us and the family that we will soon have, and the wisdom to be the best wife that I can be to him. Help me to make the proper decisions

that will best fit our lives. I ask that you give Matthew the wisdom and courage to be the head of our family and lead us in the right direction. And no matter what happens, help us to always remember to look to you for the answers to each and every one of our problems. I pray this in your name. Amen."

After I finished praying, I went to grab my sister to help me put my dress on. I was homebound for the altar.

—

The morning of our big day is finally here, and I barely slept a lick. I wonder if she had a hard time sleeping like I did. I thought about calling or texting her, but just in case she was asleep, I didn't want to wake her up. There was no need for both of us to be tired.

All night I tossed and turned from nerves and anxiety. My brother stayed the night with me, my dad and the other groomsmen would come over tomorrow morning to get dressed before we head to the church. I can't wait to see what she looks like. All night, I kept imagining the moment she walks down the aisle and how she would look. I already know she will be beautiful, but I can't wait to see her in her dress and new hairstyle. When she told me she was going to cut it, I got a little upset because I love her long hair, but she assured me it wouldn't be that much; though I'm not exactly sure what "that much" means. But whatever it turns out to be, I am sure I will still love it.

As I began to get ready, so many emotions swarmed through my head. Feelings of excitement, joy, and nerves fill my body. I never thought this day would come so soon. For many years, I've prayed and asked God to send me a wife that will love me through all my flaws and love me for who I am, not what I could be. I wanted to be married because I didn't want to enjoy my life alone. I saw my parent's marriage and how much they loved each other and immediately I knew I wanted something like that. I saw how hard they worked for everything they have. I knew it would take hard work and more, but I was willing to put in the time and work because they were truly happy. Mariah was someone I could see myself starting a family with and being happy with. Before leaving for the church, I say a little prayer:

"Lord, I ask that you guide Mariah and I's feet on this path we are about to start together. Lord, I know there will be tests and trials, and those only come to make us stronger. Through those, we will pray and trust you because you know what's best for us. I ask that you continue to give me the knowledge and wisdom to lead our family down the path of righteousness so that we may not stray away from the word but be engrossed in it. I ask that you also help me to always make the right decisions for us and when I do make a mistake, which I know will happen, that I learn from it and that you help me make it right. I know this marriage is of your will and that you'll always bless us Lord. In your name I pray, Amen."

With that, I headed for the church to begin my new life.

—

As I walked from Matthew's office to the sanctuary doors, I was overwhelmed with so many emotions I couldn't help but to cry. The doors to the sanctuary opened and everyone stood up as *Here and* Now by Luther Vandross played. That was the song Matthew wanted to be played as I walked down the aisle. My dad greeted me at the beginning of the aisle to walk me down. The walk down the aisle of the church seemed so long. I saw so many faces crying with tears of joy that I couldn't hold any of mine back. I didn't want to mess up my make-up, but soon that thought left my mind.

When I got to the altar where Matthew, the bridesmaids, and the groomsmen stood, Matthew's dad said, "Who gives this woman to marry this man?", my dad answered, "I do.", and handed me over to Matthew. And then the preacher continues, "We are gathered here today, on this happy and joyous occasion, to join this man and this woman in holy matrimony…" and so on.

When we came to the "I do's" part of the service, his dad announced that Matthew had written his own vows, in which he would read.

"Mariah, when I first met you, I would have never imagined that you would be my wife. When you came into the choir room that day and played for me and Carl, I could sense the anointing and the power of God on your life. I didn't know you very well, or even where you stood relationship wise. I wasn't brave enough to ask you on a date, especially considering I was a pastor. I didn't think you'd want to go to dinner with me. But soon enough I managed to muster up enough courage to ask you and to my surprise, you said yes. That began this long journey we are currently on. Mariah, I love you more than you would even know. You're all that and more than I could ever ask for in a woman and most of all, you're saved and love the Lord as I do. Every day I thank God that he allowed you to come into my life so that I may marry you. I can't wait to start our lives together. To start ministry together and start building a family. I feel like I've waited my whole life for you. There's so much I want to experience with you. With this ring, I give you my eternal love."

And then it was my turn.

"Matthew, I've never felt this way about a man like I do about you. It seems like no matter what the issue may be, you always have some type of answer or solution to the problem. I love how romantic you are. Just the simple things you do, like the flowers waiting on my desk in the mornings or when you bring me lunch, you make life more worthwhile. When we first met, I was nervous. I didn't expect to fall so quickly for you like I did. It felt unreal, and it still feels like I'm living in a fairytale. But the best part is every time I wake up, you're still there. It pleases me to know that I'm going to be able to spend the rest of my life with you and that we will be able to start a family together. I couldn't imagine spending my life with anyone else but with you. I love you Matthew Muleniro."

After saying our vows, the preacher announced that Matthew may now kiss the bride. Matthew and I kissed, and everyone clapped and screamed. That truly became the best day of my life.

102

Chapter 14:

Mrs. Mulinero

Soon the wedding was over, and it was off to the reception. I was so excited to sit, eat, and talk with all my family and friends. Before that, we had to take pictures, which I wasn't necessarily excited for. Even though I was all about capturing this moment to look back on, after being to a few weddings, I knew that pictures take forever. Matthew and I had our own limo to drive us to the reception which was at the Hyatt in Downtown LA. We also planned to take pictures outside of the hotel, as well. There was a garden near the walkway to the hotel that had a fountain and some benches. It was overall a really nice area to capture this moment with our wedding party.

As we drove to the hotel, Matthew and I didn't speak much. I was honestly speechless, still trying to fully grasp what just happened. All my life, I imagined what this day would be like and even how it would play out. I never imagined it would feel like this. I laid my head on his shoulder as we sat there holding hands.

To my surprise, the pictures didn't take as long as I thought it would, and by this time I felt like I was starving. After the pictures, Matthew and I checked into our hotel room at the Hyatt where I changed into my reception dress. It was similar to the bridesmaid's dresses except it was a little longer and more flowing at the bottom and it was lavender. It was nice to have that alone time with Matthew before this long eventful night we had ahead of us. I knew it would be a while before it would just be us two again.

While I changed, Matthew and I exchanged a few words about the wedding and comments that we received so far. We were both excited to see all the photos we had just taken with everyone. Once we finally got downstairs to the front desk, the hotel staff greeted us again and took us to the ballroom where everyone was waiting for us. Immediately, we sat down, and I had the waiter bring me a plate. It was around four o'clock, and I hadn't really eaten anything almost the whole day. We were both so excited to see everyone, but first on the list was something to eat. After we ate, we'd go mingle with everyone. I saw friends from college that I hadn't seen in so many years. It was so nice to be reacquainted with all of them.

While we were eating, my sister thought it would be a good time to have a few people give us good wishes on our marriage. My dad immediately jumped up and said he wanted to go first. The room soon got quiet, as he grabbed the microphone and began,

> "I always knew that one day my baby girl would get married. I always hoped that I would be here to see it. I've seen her grow up to be a beautiful, talented, young woman. When she told me about this Matthew person, I was a little skeptical, only because I didn't know him. But after so many months of Mariah telling me about him and how great he was, I thought that I'd give him a chance. Then came the day when I was able to meet him and instantly, I knew that he was the one for her. I really couldn't imagine Mariah being with anyone else because it was like Matthew was made just for her. I wish you both longevity and that you have a prosperous marriage. I love you both."

Everyone clapped and a few more people came up and expressed their love. Then it was time for the father daughter dance. The DJ put on, *If This World Were Mine* by Luther Vandross and we had our dance in the middle of the dance floor. I hadn't danced with my father in so long, that was definitely a highlight of my evening. Next up was me and Matthew's dance, we danced to, *When You Know* by Dianne Reeves. She is such a great Jazz artist and I absolutely love that song by her. I felt like I danced with Matthew forever, that quickly became our song.

After our dance, Matthew and I continued mingling with friends and family, soaking up all that we could from that night. It all seemed like a dream. I was so worried something would go wrong but everything was literally perfect. The wedding planner did such a great job bringing our vision to life. And most of all, Matthew looked so happy.

The reception soon ended, and everyone started going their separate ways home and back to their hotels. Since our flight didn't leave until tomorrow afternoon, we would spend our first night at the hotel. It was nice not having to drive anywhere when everything was over, especially after the long day we just had. As promised, Claire brought my bags to the room after the reception, and Jhana stayed and took my dress back to my house. Everything went so smooth, it felt unreal. I am so grateful to have so much help today, it made all the difference.

After countless tries, I finally got Matthew to tell me where we were going for our honeymoon. He only decided to tell me one of the two places we were going, which was Turks and Caicos. I couldn't believe he was taking me there, that was a place I dreamed of going to. I couldn't wait to go to the beach, relax and take it all in. Turks and Caicos was so beautiful and tropical. If this was just the first place, I could only imagine where the second place would be. We already had our bags packed, so all we would have to do was go to the airport and be on our way.

When we got to our room, I took a shower, changed into my silk nightgown and laid down next to my new husband. That entire night he held me, and we talked about our future. Of course, God may not have the same idea for us but it's always nice to imagine. We had so much to catch up on from the last few days of not seeing each other. One big topic was the idea of having children. He asked me how I felt about it and I told him I'd love to have children one day. But I wasn't necessarily sure if I wanted to start having them right away. I mean we are both young and had plenty of time, so there was definitely no rush. He expressed that he wanted to have children also and when I was ready, we would. We talked about wanting children earlier in our relationship, but we were still dating at that time. I remember him telling me he wanted a big family, exactly how big would be the question.

We also talked more about both of our families and how mine acted during the rehearsals before the wedding. I was hoping that this was something that wouldn't come up, but I knew that he would want an explanation about the rehearsal dinner.

"So, Cakes, your uncle seemed really upset at the dinner. What was with that?" Matthew said.

"Not really sure." I replied back.

I tried to keep answers short so this conversation wouldn't prolong.

"I sense you don't really want to talk about this, but I'd really like to know why they were arguing. Was there something else going on I didn't know about?" he asked.

"No, there wasn't anything going on. He always feels the need to be in control and when he isn't, he'll do anything to get it back. I didn't think anything of it at the time, but it probably wasn't the best idea to have the whole family there during the rehearsal. They couldn't just come to dinner, sometimes my family forgets how to act." I started to chuckle. "When he started talking, my mom tried to diffuse the situation so we could move on. I'm sorry that happened during the rehearsal." I said to him.

"I mean, I've just never seen something like that. Just like out of the blue he started getting agitated and whatnot. I thought I had done something wrong, something was wrong. I was just really confused." He replied.

"You didn't do anything wrong and it wasn't your fault. That's just how he is, and my family argues all the time about it. Welcome to our imperfect family."

"I'm sorry it has to be like that, but if that's what you come with I'll take it." He told me.

"It's not your fault. Can we talk about something else?" I said.

"Of course." He replied.

It wasn't that I didn't like talking about my family, because we all are really close, and I loved them dearly. But, just like every family, we have our ups and downs, but we somehow always manage to get through it. It's just the fact that I'd rather not disclose what arguments happen behind closed doors because some of them are embarrassing. I know being married to Matthew, he'll eventually find out some of what has happened, but just not right now. We continued our conversation about the wedding.

"So, what did you think about today?" He asked.

"I'm not even sure I can put it into words. It was amazing. I had so much fun, I felt so much love, and most of all, I officially became your wife. It all felt like a dream." I replied.

"Yeah, I felt the same way. I'll admit, I was getting a little antsy and a little stressed out not being able to see you. I know we both had some much going on, but I just wanted to see you. Even if it was just for a second. I had to know if you were dealing with everything okay. I was a little worried. Tonight, truly felt like a dream. It was more than I even imagined it would be."

"I know", I said as I looked up at him and rubbed his face. "I missed you too. I tried not to get upset cause I knew we'd be back together soon. Jhana meant well, she had activities planned for the bridal party to bond and have a good time. She just wanted us to enjoy as much of each other for as long as we could."

"I did too. We've been spending so much time together these last few months I thought I was going to lose it. I know she meant well, I wasn't used to not seeing you." He said laughing.

"But on the bright side, it was worth the wait because you looked sooooo handsome in your tuxedo."

"Why thank you." He said with the biggest smile on his face. Seeing you walk down the aisle was definitely worth the wait. I didn't even realize you were going to write your own vows too. I guess we both wanted to make the day even more special and speak from the heart."

"The wedding was perfect, the pictures were perfect, and the reception was nothing less. What was your highlight?"

"Everything was so great, like you said. It's hard to choose just one. What was yours? I needed time to think about his question.

"I was most excited for our first dance together. When you sent the me song *When You Know* after I proposed, I instantly knew I wanted that to be "our" song. I'm so glad you agreed."

"I think one of my highlights was walking down the aisle and seeing everyone's smiling faces. The room was filled with love. It felt amazing. We danced the entire night away."

"Honestly, my face hurt from smiling so much. I never imagined the day feeling like that. It's truly a night I'll never forget. You looked absolutely stunning in your dress. I almost didn't want you to take it off. You looked like a princess."

"That dress was not as comfortable as I hoped it would be." I said laughing.

"And you hardly wear makeup, but WOW. It was just all so much to take in at once."

"I'm glad you enjoyed all of it. I'll try to wear makeup more often."

"But not too often." He said, smirking.

"I love you Mr. Mulinero."

"I love you Mrs. Mulinero."

And with that, we went to sleep.

Chapter 15:

The Honeymoon

Finally, Sunday morning came, and we we're leaving to start our honeymoon. Last night was great with just Matthew and I alone, no cellphones or television. Just us two, talking with light music in the background. When we first walked into the room, I immediately noticed the rose petals on the floor leading to the bed. The room smelled like Yankee Candle's Passion Fruit Martini, I knew that was one of Matthew's favorites. I continued to walk in as Matthew put our bags down by the door. The bed was decorated with flower petals, chocolates and two towel doves with a message that said "Love is in the Air " with "M&M" right below it. I quickly realized why I was being asked all those different questions from our wedding planner earlier that week. Now I know she was working to set up our room. After settling in, I turned on some Jazz from my favorite artist Kirk Whalum. It was the perfect romantic scene.

We called a cab to take us to the airport from the hotel. Our parents offered to drive us, but we were officially checked out and on vacation. We planned to have limited communication with the outside world, to fully enjoy ourselves during our honeymoon. We both took vacation on our jobs, Matthew made sure the church was squared away for the next two weeks and everyone knew what to do since he'd be gone. He made it clear even though he'd be gone, everything was to still run as normal. This was the first time he'd be away for more than a few days and not readily available, so he was a little nervous. I assured him everyone knew their roles and it would be fine. I also wanted everything to be as smooth as possible, so we crossed all our t's before we left.

As we headed to the terminal, I became even more excited. Matthew planned our entire honeymoon. And when I say the entire honeymoon, I mean where we were going, what we were going to do, how we were going to do it, and what time. He had a very detailed itinerary, but everything was going to be a surprise. He told me to pack for a tropical place and to make sure I brought tennis shoes. All I knew is that we were going to Turks and Caicos for about a week, then we were flying someone else after that, but he wouldn't tell me where. Even though I like surprises, the suspense was killing me. I couldn't seem to shake him of what all we were going to do.

We weren't expected to land in Turks and Caicos until late that night, so I figured we probably wouldn't do much that day. When we finally arrived in Turks and Caicos, we were greeted by the lovely Island natives from the moment we got off the plane. We grabbed our bags and headed to the shuttle that would drop us off at our resort. By this time, it was seven o'clock. Matthew checked us in and told the receptionist that we reserved the honeymoon suite. She said congratulations, handed us the keys, and up the stairs we went.

The hotel was so nice. It incorporated much of the Island's tropical senses with trees in the lobby and various drinks that came in coconuts. They had a bar and multiple seating areas. There were a few restaurants where you could either sit down or order to your room and there was a huge pool right outside the lobby in between the buildings where the rooms were. And of course, the beach was close by. Our suite was just as nice as the lobby and almost as big. When you first walk in the room, there's a living room area that leads into the kitchen. Attached to the kitchen was a balcony that had a table and chairs which overlooked the beach. The bathroom had a Jacuzzi tub and a shower in it as well. It reminded me of a small apartment. I knew I was going to enjoy this.

After we got settled in the room, we went downstairs to eat at one of the restaurants before they closed. They had a good variety of food, including normal American dishes as well. I'm assuming for the tourists. What caught our eye was the long list of seafood dishes they offered. I ordered some shrimp and crab legs, and Matthew ordered the steak and lobster. The steak was prepared with local herbs and spices, so it wasn't traditional in the least bit. We'd only been here a few hours and I was sure I wouldn't be ready to go when it was time. I was enjoying myself so much, taking in all the beauty and splendor Turks and Caicos had to offer. After we ate, we went and laid on the beach for a little before heading back to the room. I was excited to take a hot bath in that Jacuzzi tub and turn in for the night.

The next morning, I woke up to breakfast in bed. Matthew woke up early and got us breakfast from the lobby, which was complimentary. He said he had a long but relaxing day planned for us, so we ate and then got dressed. He had arranged for us to go and spend the day at the spa, I was super excited about that. I mean, who doesn't love a good massage that your husband pays for? The spa took up most of that day, which was perfectly fine with me. We tried another restaurant in the hotel which turned out to be just as good as the one the night before.

The next few days began like the others. Breakfast and then a series of events in which Matthew planned. I was so surprised at how romantic he could be. We had candlelit dinners, long walks on the beach, and he bought me literally everything I wanted. Gifts, jewelry, souvenirs, you name it. He was spoiling me and I loved it. We went on a short hike, went whale watching, and did a rock climb that led to a zip line, which was probably my favorite thing we did. I was beginning to really enjoy this married life. Since our hotel room overlooked the beach, it was nice that we could walk outside and be right there. And don't forget the beautiful view we had. It was all too amazing to put into words.

Our final day in Turks and Caicos came too soon. I was excited to see where we were going next, but I wasn't sure I wanted to leave, we were in paradise. The whole trip was so much better than I thought it would be. Everything was a surprise, which made it even better. And since we had such a great time there, I knew we'd have a great time at our next destination.

We flew countless hours from Turks and Caicos to Athens, Greece. Could this honeymoon get any better? He told me he wanted us to share the experience of going to a place I wanted and a place he wanted. He always wanted to go to Greece to experience the food and all the ancient museums and monuments. I instantly saw a different side of him. His face lit up when he started talking about all the history in Greece and everything he wanted to see. He was excited and I was honored to share that moment with him.

When we arrived, it was still fairly light outside. We checked in the hotel and went on our way for some sightseeing. It felt good to get out and stretch after that long plane ride. I had no idea what day it was and spent way too much time sleeping on the plane, hoping it would make the time pass quicker. I was so exhausted from the plane ride; I wasn't sure I wanted to do anything else. But we only had a few days here and I wanted to make the best of it.

During our time there, we were able to get a tour and see all the famous landmarks. We saw some of the ancient arenas and statues like the Panathenaic Stadium, Temple of Athena Nike, the Temple of Olympian Zeus, and learned more about the ancient Greeks. They gave us brochures for almost every building and went into depth about the fights that went on in each arena and even how people would prepare for the fights and to watch them. A lot of the statues had fallen during different time periods and many of them weren't repaired or rebuilt, but the tour guides still showed us where they were and pictures of them. We tried all kinds of different foods, some I wasn't too keen about, but it was a part of the experience. We walked more than I have in my life. It was no question as to whether he cared about me because he really took the time to make sure I enjoyed myself. Our entire trip was thoughtful and planned out, and not to mention the amount of money that went into it as well. I knew our family would always be taken care of. I had such an amazing time and couldn't have asked for a better honeymoon with the man that I loved. We finished up our trip in Greece and headed home.

Chapter 16:

The Return Home

We spent about four days in Athens before heading back home to L.A. I couldn't thank Matthew enough for the amazing two and a half weeks that we just had. When I returned to work on Friday, everyone congratulated me once more and wanted to see pictures from the wedding and the honeymoon. We were still waiting on our professional photos from the photographer but of course I still took plenty with my phone. It was still hard for me to believe that all this was happening to me; it truly was the best feeling in the world. The thought of spending the rest of your life with someone that you dearly love, cherish, and care about is more that anyone could ever ask for.

I knew that Krystal, Claire, and my sister Jhana would want to know everything about the honeymoon and I didn't mind telling them. It would just be better if everyone was there at the same time, it was the perfect opportunity to have some girl time. I called Jhana that morning to see if she was free to come down for lunch. She was, so I invited Krystal and Claire to lunch to fill them all in on the scoop.

"OMG! You have to tell us what happened. I mean, how was it? What did you guys do, where did you go? Don't leave anything out," Krystal said excitingly.

"Well, calm down. I'll start from the beginning. So, after the reception, Matthew and I stayed the rest of the night at the hotel until our flight left for Turks and Caicos the next afternoon." I started.

"Turks and Caicos!!!! Are you serious? I've always wanted to go there." Jhana and Claire screamed.

"Yes, Turks and Caicos. It's so beautiful there, the people are so nice, and the men… they are something to talk about. So, Krystal, if Daniel doesn't work out you have some place to go look." I said laughing.

"Shut up," Krystal replied laughing. "Daniel ain't going nowhere, keep going now."

"Okay, okay. So, we got to the hotel and it was a resort. It was starting to get late so we checked in, settled in the room, got some dinner and went to sleep. The next day, we got breakfast from the lobby, which was delicious, and spent the day at their spa. Let me tell you, it was amazing! They have these healing incense that's supposed to help cure different health problems; such as back aches, sinus issues, and stuff. So, you sit in a steam room setting with the scents going for like an hour or so before you get the actual massage. Over the next few days, we went rock climbing and zip lining, we went on a hike, and ate great food the entire trip." I told them.

"Wow, that sounds so nice. Did he plan this all himself?" Jhana asked.

"Yes, yes he did. It was all a surprise to me. The only thing I knew was the first place we were going, but there's more." I replied back.

"Well keep going." They all said in unison. They were all invested, listening on the edge of their seats.

"Okay, well the rest of our time there, we toured the island, went to the beach almost every night and just enjoyed ourselves. Even though we did things every day we were there, it didn't seem like too much. At the same time, it was really nice to relax and get away. Then, we flew from the Turks all the way to Athens, Greece. That was the big kicker, I was so shocked. I figured Turks and Caicos would be it, and I would've been happy with that. But, Matthew always tells me to expect the unexpected, and that was definitely the unexpected." I said.

"Dang girl, this man got all kinds of tricks up his sleeve. He wasn't messing around, at all." Claire said.

"Right, that's so sweet and romantic." Jhana agreed.

"I didn't know Pastor had it in him, that's what's up." Krystal chimed in.

"I know right! I mean we got there, and we were able to tour the city, seeing some of the ancient landmarks and buildings. We saw some of the arenas where the fights took place and some statues. Then, the tour guide told us some more about the ancient history of Greece, I honestly learned so much." I chuckled. "I mean it was really nice, I was having such a great time, I didn't want to leave. Greece was the last place, then we came back home." I ended.

"Wow girl, I am so happy for you. I mean I haven't seen you so happy and enthused in a long time. It's nice to see you so captivated and cheerful like this." Jhana said.

"Yea, I agree. I haven't known you for that long, but it really seems that you and Matthew are soul mates." Krystal said.

"Well, working with her, all I hear about is Matthew. There were many days she'd come into work late because they stayed up late talking on the phone. It was so cute." Claire added.

"I agree with you all, I haven't dated a lot of people, but I honestly don't see myself with anyone else but Matthew." I replied back to them. "He really makes me happy."

"So now that you're back, what's the next move?" Krystal asked,

"Well we have to find a place to live, amid planning the wedding and everything else that was going on that fell to the bottom of the list."

"Do y'all want to buy a house?" Jhana asked

"Yeah, we're definitely going to look into that. It's probably the best bet right now." I replied.

"And what about kids?" Jhana asked.
The entire wedding preparation, she kept talking nonstop about how she couldn't wait for a niece or nephew, she was worse than our parents.

"No Jhana. We're not having kids right now." I replied laughing. "Soon enough, but we want to enjoy being married for a while."

"Okay, Okay. I'll accept that." She replied, but I could tell she wasn't satisfied with that answer.

As much as I wanted to stay and chat with them, I had to leave after our conversation and head back to work. Being gone for almost three weeks really took a toll on my job, I had a lot of paperwork and filing to do, as well as some offers for some new cases. On top of that, Matthew and I needed to start looking for a house. Currently, we were still in our separate homes and hadn't figured out living arrangements. He had a condo which wouldn't hold us for long, and I had a house that would be big enough for the meantime, but didn't have a lot of extra rooms for when we wanted to start a family. We talked about buying a home together during our honeymoon, so that part was set. We were so focused on enjoying our time together, that we never made any definite plans. In the meantime, I figured we'd stay at my house so he could close his lease. I bid them goodbye before leaving to finish my workday then start my weekend.

That Monday, I got to work a little early since there was still so much that I had to do. We wanted to start looking at houses as soon as possible, so I had my paralegal look for some real estate agents. Luckily, she found a few, in which I talked to and was able to set up a few showings for that day. We weren't in a big rush to find a house, but the sooner the better to get that part of our lives closed. I also still needed to catch up on the paperwork and finalize a case I started before I left. I didn't get much done Friday between the long lunch date I had with the girls and sorting through all the emails I had. Claire was able to get a lot done while I was gone, but there were still documents I needed to sign off on before they could be completed. I figured I'd work late for the next few days just to catch up on everything.

I called Matthew to tell him about the showings I set up.

"Hey sweetie, Claire found a few real estate agents and one had some bookings for today around four o'clock. Are you able to go?" I asked him.

"Yeah, I'll be there." he replied.

"OK." I said back.

The agent ended up showing us two houses, both were nice but the second house we looked at had everything I wanted in a dream home. The house was big, much bigger than we needed right now but I was pretty set on it. It had three floors, with eight bedrooms, four and a half bathrooms, 5 on the top floor and 3 in the basement, half bath on the main floor, lots of closet space, and a finished basement with a bar and small movie theater room. The kitchen was also big with a double oven, an island in the middle and a nice size area for a dining room table. The best thing about it was that it had just been built and we were the first ones to look at it after it was put back on the market. They told us the first owners pulled out right before they were about to close, so they had to sell the house at a lower value since the new owners wouldn't be able to pick all the upgrades they wanted. It almost didn't make sense not to make an offer, so I figured we better jump on top of it, fast.

When we were finished looking at the houses, there were a few things we needed to discuss with the realtor. We also had to sign some paperwork to get everything started. After that was finished, we headed over to his condo to finish packing up his stuff. Our wedding and honeymoon didn't come at a better time because his lease was up, and he had to move anyway. This would be the best time for us to start purging our stuff and moving his stuff over to my house. Since we'd be buying a new home soon, it made more sense to start packing now to prevent a hassle later. We spent the rest of our night packing and cleaning.

Chapter 17:

Our Beginning

A few weeks have passed, as we continue the process of buying the house we want. I convinced Matthew to purchase the second house. He liked the first house we saw, which was much smaller than the second one. But overall, the second house was cheaper and came with a better deal. He eventually caved in and the relator was able to get some of the final processing fees waived, which brought the price down further. We were finally able to buy our dream home and begin to move in and I was super excited. There were so many new things happening; the marriage, new husband, new house, and now the new move. Things couldn't be going any better.

It was now mid-July and we were all moved in with the new furniture on its way. We even hired a professional designer to come in and decorate the house. It was Matthew's idea to bring one in, and I decided to go with it. I was able to help her pick all the furnishings and decorations which really turned out nice. Since we were all settled in the new house, Matthew wanted to celebrate with a nice home cooked meal. While we were dating, he told me his parents made sure all their children knew how to cook, not just the girls. It was common that Italians taught both the men and women how to cook in the household. This was something that was important to Matthew's parents. They wanted their children to be well rounded adults and to them cooking a meal had no gender. He made chicken parmesan with homemade pasta sauce, he never bought pre-made sauce from the store. I also hadn't even realized it was our three-month anniversary of being married, time really seemed to be flying by.

Things really started to pick up at the office also. I was now working on those two cases that were on my desk when I came back from my honeymoon all while still closing a few cases I had before the wedding. I was really busy and found myself spending a lot of extra time at the office. It was hard because I wanted to be home even though I couldn't. Now it was different since I had a husband waiting at home for me. Before, it would just be Paulo waiting at home, needless to say, he could survive without me for a few hours. I tried not to stay longer than I needed, but I somehow always found a way to work it all out.

Work was busy, but I had to stay home today… I haven't been feeling well for the last few days, but today it was unbearable. I did a little work at home, but it wasn't the same as being in the office. I didn't have access to all the files I needed and communicating with Claire over the phone wasn't super-efficient. I never really worked from home before, so I didn't have all the tools I needed to get everything done. I tried my best to nurse myself back to health with the remedies from my childhood. Maybe it was what I was eating, on top of all the stress and change from my job. But slowing down didn't change how I felt, and I couldn't figure out what was wrong. Some days I felt okay and others I didn't want to leave the bed. I would wake up with fevers and have stomach aches all throughout the day. Even Matthew started to get worried, I couldn't take it anymore, so I just decided to go to the doctor and figure out what was wrong.

I called Wednesday morning and was able to get an appointment the same day. I got to the doctor's office 15 minutes early to do the regular check in. The nurse asked me why I was seeing the doctor and after I told her my symptoms, she said they would have me take a pregnancy test as well. Once I got back to the room it was time to play the waiting game. I sat there anxiously waiting for the test results.

While waiting, I kept replaying the last few months, even few months back in my mind to see if I could actually be pregnant. I was having normal pregnancy symptoms plus more, so I thought it was a flu or some type of sickness. When the doctor came back in, she confirmed the test was positive and ordered an ultrasound to see how far along I was. I had the option to wait about 45 minutes for the ultrasound or come back another day for an appointment. I decided to wait since I was already there. We went over the typical pregnancy do's and don'ts. She also asked me a lot of questions about my diet, exercise and sleeping schedule. She informed me the first trimester is often the most critical because that is when the placenta is developing and my body would be working extra hard to begin accommodating the baby. She gave me a list of good foods to eat and medicines I could take while pregnant. I was still in disbelief, and now feeling overwhelmed with all the information. By the time she finished with all the questions and information, the nurse practitioner came in to do the ultrasound.

I was shocked when she told me that I was about ten weeks pregnant. I couldn't help but cry when I heard the baby's heartbeat. I was overjoyed and instantly fell in love. Pregnancy never came to my mind when I was throwing up, but that would explain why I was feeling sick. I thought it was just because I was working so much these past couple of weeks and needed a break. We were both so busy and there were so many changes happening, I stopped paying attention to my health. I know Matthew and I talked about waiting to have children, but I guess God had other plans for us. I left the doctor's office feeling amazing, I knew Matthew would be so excited and I couldn't wait to tell him at our dinner date later that night. I figured this would be a great night to revisit our favorite spot, Le Lieu Du Déjeuner.

"Hey sweetie, how was work?" he asked.

"It was okay, I just went to the office for a few hours before my doctor's appointment." I replied back.

"Oh, yeah. How did it go? What did they say?" he asked.

"Well… she told me everything was okay and…", I paused before continuing. "...and, that I was pregnant." I said smiling.

"ARE YOU SERIOUS?!" He screamed, jumping out of his chair.

"Yes, I'm serious. Can you sit down?" I whispered to him, as everyone began to look at us in the restaurant.

"I'm sorry, I'm just so excited. Have you called your parents yet?" He started firing off questions.

"No, not yet. I wanted you to be the first to know. I'll call them tonight when we get home."

"Oh, wow Mariah! I mean, I don't even know what to say. We're going to have a baby in a matter of months. There's so much we have to do. Buy clothes, a bed, and decorate the room. We can have the lady who decorated the house come back and help, she did such a good job. You know she comes highly recommended…" Matthew continued to rant.

"Yes Hun, I know." I interrupted him laughing. "We have plenty of time for decorations. Besides, we don't even know the sex of the baby. I'm really excited too! Doc told me about these baby yoga classes that we can go to and they teach you about the different positions you can give birth in, breathing exercises, and things like that. They are on Wednesdays and Fridays at 4:00 and 6:00 p.m. I think we should go, we would only need to go once a week."

"Yeah, sure, anything. Whatever you want."

"And don't worry, you won't be the only man there. They recommend partners to come also."

"Oh okay. That makes me feel a little better." He said smiling. "I mean I would still go because you wanted me but knowing I won't be the only man there gives me some relief.

"Awe, that's sweet. You'd come just because I asked you." I said blushing.

"Yes, I would, because I love you."

"And I love you too."

We left the restaurant, both feeling on top of the world. I had to call my mom and dad to let them know the great news as well.

"Hey Mom, is Dad there with you?" I asked her.

"Yeah, let me get him on the phone." She said back.

"Wait, I want to talk to both of you." I said to her before she handed him the phone.

"Ok, we are both here." They both said.

"Okay, well I have some news for both of you. Mom, dad, well… I'm pregnant!!" I screamed.

"OMG!" I had to pull the phone away because my mom started screaming.

"Awe baby girl, I'm so happy for you. We're going to be grandparents." My dad said in his thick Korean accent.

"Yea, you guys will be. Matthew jumped out of his chair in the restaurant. Everyone started looking over at us. I had to tell him to calm himself." I said laughing.

"Well, what did you expect? Of course, he was going to be happy." My mom replied back laughing.

"Well, I knew that. I just didn't know he was going to scream like he did." I said laughing.

"I know sweetie. Well, we are so excited for you. I don't even know what to say." My mom said.

"Yes hunny, we'll come and visit you soon. We're really happy for you. I hate to rush off the phone, but I have to go to the hospital. I'm on call tonight." My dad said.

"It's ok. I understand. I love you both and I'll talk to you later." I said.

"Okay baby. Love you too." They both said and that ended our conversation.

Matthew was so excited he called all of his family to tell them the news, while I called my sister and Krystal. Everyone was so happy for us. I felt so much love from all of them. I knew he'd finish telling everyone tomorrow at rehearsal.

—

I couldn't believe I was going to be a father. When we talked about waiting to have children, I couldn't help but think what it would be like when we finally did. I'm glad we bought our house when we did, or it may have been too much for her later on. When we returned from the honeymoon, we got so busy and overwhelmed with everything. I wasn't sure about buying the house we're in, but the time couldn't have been better. Nonetheless, everything worked out the way it was supposed to. I called my parents and my sister to tell them the big news. My parents were so excited and couldn't wait to come back and visit. This would be their first grandchild and they were clear in letting me know they would spoil him or her. It was okay because I knew I would spoil them too. I couldn't wait to give them the world. Eden was ecstatic to be an aunt, she has already started referring to the baby as "auntie's baby". I was sure my child would receive so much love. I can't wait to be a father.

—

I went to work the next day feeling crappy, but there wasn't much that I could do about it. After dinner last night, Matthew and I went to the store and stocked up on ginger ale and saltine crackers. We also got some lemons, green tea, and lemon ginger tea. The doctors told me having a cup of lemon ginger tea in the morning could help with nausea and morning sickness. Matthew was kind enough to make me a cup this morning before I left for work. But, I was still feeling the effects of the morning sickness.

Time seemed to go by slowly at work, even though I was busy most of the day. It had been a while since I'd attended a rehearsal at the church, so I decided to leave a little work a little early and head to the church. I had gone to a few practices when we returned from the honeymoon, but I haven't been consistent since before the wedding. I owed it to the praise team and myself to get back to the regular groove of things.

When I arrived at the church, I was greeted with the normal "hellos" and "praise the lord first lady", a nickname that was given to me after Matthew and I got married. I headed to Matthew's office to see if he was there, to my surprise here came Krystal screaming down the foyer. She ran up to me saying, "Congrats love, OMG! I'm so happy for you!" It wasn't long before a few other saints came up to us saying they heard the news and congratulations. I didn't have time to respond to Krystal because I was so excited and overwhelmed, but I finally managed to thank everyone. After I spoke to everyone, I walked into Matthew's office and he got up and kissed me hello.

"What was all that commotion outside?" he asked.

"Well Krystal started it." I said laughing. "She ran up to me and said congratulations and other saints came up to do the same. Sorry to disrupt you." I said back.

"Oh, you didn't. I was just wondering what was going on. How was work today?" he asked.

"It was okay. Long, but okay. I'm starving got some food?" I asked him.

"Yeah, because I just keep random meals in my office." He said sarcastically.

"Ok smarty, I was just asking." I said back.

"No, I don't. We can grab something afterward."

"Ok. Maybe you should keep some snacks in here for us. And by us, I mean me and the baby." I said laughing.

He looked up and smiled back.

It felt so good to get back into the groove of things. Since I have been missing so many rehearsals, I don't always play during service anymore, which is something I have been missing. I don't feel comfortable playing, not knowing the songs or what's going on. Carl always changes things to make the songs a little more original. I would do my best to follow along, but other times I didn't bother. It's also nice to enjoy the service too, and not always be a part of it. Matthew knew how much playing piano meant to me and how happy it made me. In some instances, it also kept me sane. So, when he saw me in rehearsal, he couldn't help but smile back. He sat there and watched the entire time. I even forgot about how crappy I was feeling.

—

It's been a few months since Mariah went to a rehearsal and I could tell she was ready to get back to it. I sat there during the rehearsal, which I don't normally do, watching her smile and laugh with everyone. You can tell they really missed her. I love the way her face lights up when she's playing, such a glow comes over her when she's up there. It's like she goes into a zone with just her and God. I'm hoping with life calming down a little, she'll be able to be there more consistently. We were slowly starting to find a groove and as soon as we did, Mariah finds out she's pregnant. Even though it's good news, we'll have to adjust again. I'm sure that won't stop her from playing though. I just hope the pregnancy doesn't put too much of a strain on her. I've learned over this past year in dating her that she doesn't know when to slow down or stop. She was so overworked during the wedding planning and got upset when I told her she needed to calm down. Now with the pregnancy, she won't have a choice to not overdo things. I would make sure she was getting enough rest. I love watching her in action. You can tell she has so much fun being on that organ. And her voice! Who would have ever thought she could sing too? Something she was hiding from everyone. I know she looks forward to playing at service every week, and so do I.

Chapter 18:

Baby Plus 1?

I finally feel like I am balancing everything. I was almost done with the two cases I was working on, which was great. I now have some free time to prepare for this baby and spend more time with my husband. I'm trying to get everything under as much control as I can now. After the baby comes I won't take on multiple cases at once or most of my free time would be gone. Even though I enjoyed staying busy, I figured it would be more beneficial to use the extra time to get everything done that we needed to. And I knew Matthew wouldn't let me take on multiple cases at once while being pregnant, especially if I began to get more tired.

It seems like my belly began to get bigger and bigger by the day. Most of my life, I have been very petite, and then one day I wasn't anymore. I kept thinking I should be a little smaller for 14 weeks, but they do say everyone carries their pregnancies differently. It was both weird and cool to know that another human was growing inside me. There were a lot of changes happening to my body. It was such a different experience for me knowing that a woman's body could endure all of this. Matthew was always there to comfort me and reassure me everything that was happening how it was supposed to. He always knew what to say to make me feel better.

The time came quickly for my 17-week check-up. It was Wednesday and Matthew got off early so that he could go also. I was getting an ultrasound and he didn't want to miss it. He was so excited to be able to see the baby for the first time. This was the first ultrasound I had after finding out I was pregnant so it would probably be a long one. We got to the doctor's office and did the routine check in, we waited a while before the doctor came into the room.

"Hello all, how's everything going?" Doctor Sanders asked.

"Everything is going really great!" I replied back.

"That's really good to hear. How are you feeling about everything?

"Well, I'm still a little nervous, but very excited. My body has changed so much in these last few weeks and my stomach has grown!" I started to laugh.

"It sure has, but that's all normal. Everyone carries their pregnancy differently and that includes the amount of weight you gain as well. Let's take a look at the baby."

"Ok." Matthew and I replied.

She reached over to grab the fetal doppler which is used to hear the baby's heartbeat. She placed it on my stomach and started to move it around. In a matter of seconds, she began to get a funny look on her face.

"Umm, is everything ok doc?" I asked.

"Uh", she paused, "Yes, it is. I just thought I heard something. Let's do the ultrasound." She replied.

I started to get worried because I thought the baby may not have been there. Could I have miscarried? I mean, what could be the reason why she was looking that way? Soon we began the ultrasound, and I could see the baby, so everything in that aspect was okay. But, that still didn't explain the look on her face from earlier. She started showing us the baby and where its head and everything was. We could see the heart beating and where the lungs were. We both started to get excited again. Everything began to set in; I was actually carrying a human being. After she pointed to a few of the limbs, she told me to lay on my side. All the excitement caused me to forget how she responded earlier when she first listened to the heartbeat. I was still somewhat confused. After I turned on my side, it seemed as though she began to look for something.

"Ok, doc what's going on? I'm getting worried here." I asked her.

"I'm sorry, nothing is wrong. I just thought I heard two heart beats and I'm trying to see if there is someone else in there we don't know about." She replied.

"Umm, two heart beats?!" I replied, shocked. I sat up from the bed and she jumped.

"Can you lay back down please?" She said laughing.
I laid back down on the table, secretly hoping she misheard.

"Just one second… there they are." She said.

She pointed to the screen where you could clearly see two bodies. I nearly jumped off the table again, I am already nervous for one baby. And now finding out we're having two! What have I gotten myself into? As I looked over at Matthew, my heart started beating fast. Matthew had the biggest grin on his face. I remember him telling me that there were several sets of twins in his family, both his dad and grandfather were twins; and his uncle, the twin of his dad, had twin boys as well. I was sure he was ecstatic finding this out. Meanwhile, I was still trying to process what she just told us.

"Ok, we all can clearly see, there are two babies in there meaning you are going to have twins. We're going to take some different proceedings now that we know there's two little ones in there and not just one." She told us.

"Different proceedings, like?" Matthew asked.

"Nothing bad, just viewing other options of giving birth such as the Cesarean Section. Twins don't normally go full term, so we will have to watch for that. We'll also have to give a different dose of vitamins, so both babies can get as much nourishment as possible. One twin is always born smaller than the other, so that will help offset their weights a little. I know this is a lot to give you at once, but good thing we found the second baby now as opposed to later in the pregnancy and risk losing him or her." Doc said.

"No, I'm glad you found them both too. I'm just a little shocked at all this, sort of excited, but more shocked." I said laughing.

"I would imagine, let's get you all cleaned up. I'll print the pictures for you and get your new prescriptions." She said.

"Ok." I said.

She gave me some towels to wipe the gel off my stomach and left the room to get the paperwork. Matthew instantly hugged me and said how excited he was. He couldn't believe we were going to have twins, especially since there were so many sets of twins in his family. We talked about having twins earlier in our relationship, but I never thought it would actually happen. After he let me go, he instantly saw the worry on my face. This was so much to process at once. How would I take care of two babies? I mean I would obviously have to figure it out, but I was scared. I knew having Matthew there with me would make it easier, but it was all happening so fast.

"Babe, I can see the worry on your face, I want you to know that everything will be okay. Remember God will not give you more than you can bear." he said while caressing my lower back.
"God never gives you more than you can bear. I just kept repeating that to myself." The doctor finally came back to give me my new prescriptions and paperwork. We went to the desk to schedule the next appointment and then headed home. We left the doctor's office feeling happy.

—

Wow! Who could be more blessed? Within a matter of a year, I met and married the woman of my dreams, bought a beautiful house, and now we're about to have twins. What more could any man ask for? I couldn't be happier! It's hard to believe that I've accomplished so much in just a short amount of time. I knew that I always wanted to be married, but I assumed God had more work for me to do before I settled down. I know that Mariah is upset, but I did my best to assure her everything will be okay. I also let her know we were in this together and I wouldn't leave her. I promised to help as much as I could and do my best to make things as easy as I could for her. All I want to do is make my wife as happy as she can be, and with the help of God, I know that I can do all that and more.

Chapter 19:

We've Got Catching Up To Do

After we arrived home Matthew made dinner, while I took a nap. All the excitement from the doctor's appointment wore me out. We finished our night watching movies until we both fell asleep.

It was Thursday and I was super excited. I was meeting Jhana for lunch later and I couldn't wait to tell her the update. Since I was obviously showing now, I know she'll be excited to see as well. Aside from that, it was going to be a busy day. I had several meetings throughout the day at work, then lunch with Jhana. After lunch, I had to meet Matthew at the church to sign some papers, then back to work to finish the day. On top of all that, today was Thursday which meant choir rehearsal and bible study. I also had to figure out what to eat for dinner. I had just left the house and thinking about the day made me want to turn around and get back in the bed. This seemed like a coffee type of day, so I stopped by Café' Noir, a coffee shop on my way to work and got an Iced Chai Latte.

When I got to work, Claire gave me the rundown of the day. It wasn't going to be as busy as I thought. We had three meetings, two before lunch and one before it was time to head out for the day. Most of the hard work would be done in the morning, so I knew that if I could make it to lunch time and still be ok, I could make it through the rest of the day. I was really excited to have lunch with my sister and catch up on things. The two meetings made the day go by quickly, and soon it was time to meet Jhana for lunch. We went to The Palm, a high-end steak and seafood restaurant in downtown LA.

"OMG! Look at you!" Jhana screamed as she saw me walk up to the table.

"I know, I know. I didn't tell you, I have great news. We're having twins!" I replied as I sat down.

"No, you didn't tell me!" she screamed again

"First off, can we stop all the screaming? And that's probably because we just found out yesterday. I haven't even told Mom and Dad yet.

"Sorry", she apologized, but laughing, "You should. You know they are going to be ecstatic.

"I know. I'm starting to get really excited myself."

"Starting?" she questioned.

"I mean, I was really happy when I found out I was pregnant, but I was really scared. It was just so much going through my mind at once."

"Like what though? Isn't this what you wanted?" she replied.

"It's exactly what I wanted. I just felt like it was too soon. I guess I wasn't prepared to have children so early in our marriage. I was stuck on the idea of us waiting at least a year. After I told Matthew and saw his reaction, I was okay because I knew I wouldn't be alone. And then yesterday when she told us I was pregnant with two babies, I started having mixed emotions again. Like what was I going to do with two babies?"

"Umm, take care of them", she said laughing. "I'm just messing, but I'm pretty sure all moms get nervous and everything when they find out they're having a baby… or two. And with you being a first-time mom and all, there's so much for you to experience. Everything you're experiencing is normal, and you're right, you're not alone. Matthew is amazing and I'm sure he'll make a wonderful dad."

"You are absolutely right. Matthew has been extremely supportive this far. I can't wait until I can feel them moving inside. Everyone said that it feels so cool."

"You are so blessed, I'm so excited for you. I'm going to have two nieces or two nephews, or a niece and a nephew."

"I suppose that you will". I said sarcastically

"Are you guys going to find out the sex of the babies?" she asked.

"I believe so. I mean Matthew is already trying to call the decorator and what not to paint the baby's rooms. We don't even know what we are having, and he wants to paint the rooms already." I replied laughing.

"Wow, he must be pretty excited."

"Excited is an understatement; more like joyful, thrilled, and jubilant. That describes him more".

"Well, it's his first two babies!!" She screamed laughing.

"Yeah, I know, I'm letting him have his fun; I think it's cute. He's always rubbing my stomach and rubbing my feet. He gets me everything I want and puts up with my many cravings. He doesn't even complain when I get upset or anything."

"Well, it's his job to take care of you and make sure you're okay."

I agree and he's doing it very well. Now, enough about me, let's switch the subject to you."

"To me?" She said shocked.

"Yes you. I tell you everything about me and there are some things I'm still in the dark on about you."

"Like?"

"You know…" I paused before continuing. "Like this mystery man you always seem to mention but never go in depth about.

"Oh, Patrick you mean." She replied with a smirk.

"Yes, Patrick." I said laughing.

"Well, I mean. What is there to tell? We date and stuff but that's about it."

"Oh no, you're not getting off that easy. "We just date and stuff". What is "and stuff"?" I say with air quotes.

"I like him a lot, he's really sweet and all."

"And what's, "and all"." I ask her.

"And all?" She questions. "He makes me really happy, he cares for me, and he respects the way I feel and my morals. He's never pressured me to do anything I didn't want, and I respect him for that".

"Wow, that's great! I mean, he sounds like a cool kind of dude, but the fact that I haven't met him yet… makes me a little worried. Tell me more about him. What is his occupation? What does he like to do for fun?"

"He's an Investment Banker, so he works with stocks and bonds and everything like that. He also helps others invest their money. He has similar interests like me. He likes church and he goes with me every Sunday".

"Is he saved?"

"Not quite yet. I'm still working on that" She said looking down.

"Well, what does that mean?"

"It means that he has accepted Christ into his life, but I don't think he really has gone the extra mile to get saved and all that. I want him to be at least on my level before I get serious with him. I want my husband to be saved like me."

"Yes, we both do", I replied laughing.

Time passed as we continued talking about each other's significant others.

"As much as I would love to continue to chat with you, I've got to get over to the church, and then back to work."

"Okay, it's been real. Oh, and is someone already going to plan your baby shower because I would love to." she asked.

"Umm, I hadn't even thought of that, I would love it if you planned it."

"Then it's settled, I'll take care of everything."

"Thanks Hun. I appreciate that, I love you."

"I love you too."

I hugged her and we parted our separate ways.

I made my way through lunchtime traffic to the church to meet Matthew and quickly left him to get back to work. By this time, it was around 2:30pm and I was ready to call it quits. Since finding out about the twins, my energy seemed to leave quicker. I've always heard pregnant women sleep a lot and that was literally all I wanted to do. I had to go back to the office and finish up a few things before rehearsal tonight. Two more hours and I could be free.

By the time 4:30 rolled around, I was rushing to get out of the office. I was a few minutes late to rehearsal, but everyone was still getting settled in, so it was okay. Today's song agenda was *Holy Will* by The Clark Sisters and *Speak to My Heart* by Donnie McClurkin. Both of those were on the list of my favorite songs and I was looking forward to playing them.

Everyone on the praise team came prepared knowing all their notes and words which made rehearsal go by quickly. Even though rehearsal wasn't long, I was exhausted and ready to go. After rehearsal, I decided to go head home and rest while Matthew stayed to do bible study. He told me he'd pick something up for dinner on his way home. Those words were music to my ears. I drove home, changed, and took my spot on the couch as I waited for my husband to come home.

Chapter 20:

The Romance Continues

By the time Matthew got home, I had fallen asleep on the couch. I hadn't eaten yet, since I was waiting for him and I'm glad he woke me up.

"Hey Cakes. Sorry it took me so long to get back. I brought your favorite".

He always knew how to make me happy. One of my favorite meals from my favorite restaurant. Qdoba, chicken bowl, white rice, black beans, with queso, sour cream, cheese, and corn.

"Thank you, baby." I sat up while he grabbed a fork from the kitchen.

On top of being tired, I was super hungry. After we ate, I stayed up a little while to unwind with Matthew and talk about our day. He always made it a point to talk before bed and spend some time together. Especially, since we both work during the day and didn't always get to talk as much. We started this while we were dating.

"So, how was your day?" He asked while we laid on the couch.

"It was good. I had a lunch date with Jhana. She was so excited to hear about the twins."

"Wow, I'm so glad to hear that. I told my parents today too, and my dad was completely shocked. He didn't think any of us would have twins"

"Between you and your siblings? I asked.

"Yes, siblings, cousins, anyone. He was happy the gene was still going.

"I'm honored we get to carry it on." I said with a smile. "That reminds me, I need to tell my parents." I was beginning to get tired. I planned to call them tomorrow.

"You look tired. Let's get you to bed, I'll clean this up." Matthew got up and grabbed my hand, walked me upstairs and tucked me in. Never would I thought I'd love the feeling of being tucked in as an adult. I felt so safe and vulnerable at that moment. There was nowhere in the world I would have rather been. I fell asleep before he even left the room. I was secure.

I woke up the next morning looking forward to another long day. I knew I had a series of meetings pertaining to the cases I was working on. It was Friday and I was excited for the weekend because I knew I needed the rest. I was up an hour and a half earlier than normal, and after trying to go back to sleep countless times, I decided to get up and start my day. I didn't feel very well, and I hoped the sickness wouldn't carry throughout the day. I knew I'd be busy and wouldn't be able to leave early.

The bright side of that was I was almost finished with the two cases, which weirdly turned out to be one big case. A man was accused of raping and beating a 16-year-old girl and I was on the prosecuting side with the family. The court clerk filed both the charges separately and lucky enough, I received both cases. That made everything much simpler and it was easier combining the charges. It was somewhat of a tough case, but I was proud to have won. He got 25 years in jail with no parole and no chance of an early release. The girl knew the man who assaulted her, in which the defense thought that gave him cause to violate her. Their side wasn't very strong, but they did their best to paint the guy as a model citizen. The charge was just a minor slip up he had in his perfect life. Once the defense realized their case was starting to fall apart and the jury wasn't buying it, they met with me and the family to try to arrange a plea bargain. Her family wasn't too thrilled about this and wanted him to get the highest sentence he could get. They had the best lawyer on their side, so there was no need to take a plea bargain so close to our win. The family was pretty happy and so was I, I enjoy putting away the bad guys.

I had one last meeting with the family to wrap everything up and have them sign the final closing paperwork. Throughout the meeting, they kept thanking me for helping put away the man who assaulted their daughter. I let them know they were very welcome and assured them it made me just as happy to put him away. No one deserved what she went through, and with him being in jail, he couldn't hurt anyone else. I also let them know it was my pleasure to assist them.

I recently started doing some work with the LA DA's office with a program called H-TIN, which stands for Helping Those in Need. The program works with local attorneys all over Los Angeles to provide quality legal assistance to underprivileged families at an affordable cost; and they were one of those families. A court liaison works with the attorneys and the families on a price that would suffice both parties. Many lawyers even do Pro Bono work as well. I saw it as an opportunity to help others, expand my reputation and get my name out there. They have been bringing in steady clients so far, but I know criminal law cases are sometimes drawn out.

After I finished the meeting with the family, it was around three-thirty. It turned out to be a long day and I was ready for some rest. Since I had some free time, I decided to call Matthew.

"Hey sweetie. Are you busy?" I said.

"Never too busy for you. What's up?" he replied.

"Nothing much. Just wanted to hear your voice."

"Oh, that's sweet. I love hearing your voice too. How are you feeling? I know that you were a little sick this morning."

"I feel a little better. I've been sipping on ginger ale, so I won't throw up here. I have a few more hours left to go."

"Why don't you just leave early? I mean if you're done with everything, it's Friday." He said.

"Yeah, I am. I guess I could leave. I have to go to the store and get some stuff for dinner though. We have no food." I replied.

"How about we meet at the house in 30 minutes and we can go to the store together, and I'll cook tonight, so you can rest."

"Sounds like a plan. See you in a few."

"Ok."

That night, Matthew made us some authentic Italian food. His grandparents own their own meat plant in Italy, and they send us different meats every so often. All of their meat is farm raised and doesn't contain any extra chemicals. It's expensive getting everything shipped here, but worth it because the taste doesn't compare. Matthew made Penne with Italian Meatballs, everything was homemade from the sauce to the noodles. He hardly ever bought pre-made pasta or sauce from the store. It was also really nice outside, so we ate dinner on our back patio and after dinner, we decided to go on a walk through our neighborhood holding each other's hands and enjoying the breeze. You could hear the calm wind blowing behind us and our footsteps slowly syncing in time against the pavement. We didn't talk much, which made it much more special. When we returned home, we sat and watched the sunset on our porch. It was such a beautiful sight as he held me in his arms. I laid on his chest with his arms wrapped around me.

It took a little while longer for me to get to sleep that night. I guess Matthew's dinner didn't agree with me very much, or the babies by that means. The food tasted good going down, but rumbled in the stomach until it came back up. I was glad that tomorrow was Saturday, so if I didn't get much sleep tonight, I had nothing else to do but rest tomorrow. Those are the days I enjoyed the most, just Matthew and I doing absolutely nothing but being together.

Chapter 21:

Trouble in Paradise

I'm almost at the end of my first trimester and things are going well. The babies are on the right growth track and my stomach was beginning to stretch. I started googling ways to help with the itching and stretch marks. Everywhere I read, it said to moisturize. I made sure to always keep coconut oil and shea butter on hand. I moisturized my stomach every day and night; it helped so much with the itching. I couldn't feel the babies kicking yet, which was something Matthew and I were looking forward to. But the doctor said we had plenty of time, so I wasn't too concerned. Almost every night, Matthew rubs my stomach, I'm assuming in hopes of feeling something. But I always remind him we still have a way to go. I love his enthusiasm for the pregnancy. He wants to be just as close to the babies as I am. He loves lying on my stomach, and when we go to sleep, he talks to the babies. I'm not sure if they really hear him but it makes him feel closer to them. He always makes sure I'm okay and that I have everything I need. He told me he wanted to help and take as much pressure off as he could.

It was Saturday morning, and I was feeling a little better, so I decided to make Matthew and I some breakfast before he had to go to the church to do some work. We enjoyed some eggs, bacon, pancakes, apple and orange juice. While Matthew was out working, I thought that I'd enjoy the day at the spa. Seeing as I haven't been since before the wedding. It was his treat, which was even better. I was especially excited about the prenatal massage I was going to get. It was a special massage tailored to pregnant women. My doctor let us know this was an option available to use during the pregnancy and even recommended a place for me to go. I couldn't wait to get in there.

After my short spa day, I called Matthew to see if he was still at the church. He told me was going to pick something up for lunch and he'd meet me at home. He sounded a little different on the phone, but I'd figured he had to do with the church. Once I got home, I noticed that Matthew seemed a little tenser than when he left the house. We sat down at the table and I asked him what was wrong.

"Is everything ok?" I asked Matthew.

"Yea, I guess so, just a little stressed out." He answered.

"Why? What happened?"

It took a minute for him to respond. He seemed as though he didn't want to talk about it. So, I didn't press the issue too much. I thought he'd come around soon enough. Shortly after, he responded.

"I was just at the church with Daniel and we were looking at the church's bank statements and offering numbers and they aren't adding up." He said.

"Well, what exactly does that mean?" I replied.

"It means that either someone is counting the offering wrong or someone is stealing from the church. And I'm not happy with either of those. We need that money for the church's bills and expenses. With the number of members that we have, everything is supposed to work out to some extent, and it's not."

"Can't we just put the money back from our own pockets?"

"Yes, eventually that's what I'll have to do, but I still need to figure out what is going on. I mean, if you have the audacity to steal from the church, that is stealing from God. If they needed help, all they had to do was ask. We can help them, that's what I'm here for. And if I can't help, I would find someone who can"

"I know Matthew, I know. You can't worry about that. You know that God will make a way. And he will get whoever is stealing if that's what is going on. He can get them far better than you ever could. Just pray and God will lead you in the right direction. It will all work out, baby. I know this."

"I believe you. I mean I know that he will, but it just angers me that someone would do that."

"How do you know for sure someone is stealing though? Maybe it's an honest mistake." Since he was talking, I figured I kept asking questions. I couldn't imagine anyone stealing from the church, but if they were how would we know unless it was coming out of the bank?

"I'm pretty sure the offering is being counted right because I double check it, so what else could it be? The numbers are always different from what gets written down before it's handed to me."

"Change things around. Maybe have someone else lift the offering for a few weeks and see if something different happens. It will all work out, don't worry about it too much. Pray and put it in God's hands."

We ended the conversation there, even though I could tell he was still upset and thinking about it. I had to admit, it was a little bothersome. Why would anyone want to do that? And like he said, if they needed help, they could've simply asked. Matthew always stressed that his ministry was built off helping those in need. He'd go over and beyond to make sure they got the help they needed. Money was no different, so I know he was disappointed. At this point, I was exhausted and wanted to take a nap. We went upstairs and he started to rub my stomach, which was something that seemed to calm him. Maybe this time he'll feel something move back.

The weekend seemed to go by so fast. Before I knew it, it was eight thirty in the morning on Sunday and it was time to get ready for church. Today, I felt better than I have in the past few days, so, I was excited for church. But I wasn't so sure about Matthew. With the offerings coming up short, I knew he'd be on the lookout once the time came. He wasn't his normal happy self this morning. I knew he was still upset so I let him have some space while we got ready. I just wanted him to have a good time and enjoy church like usual. We got to the church a bit early, of course to open it and get everything ready. But I think he got there a bit earlier for another reason. I wasn't sure what it was and I didn't want to bring the topic up. He seemed to be having a good day and I wanted to keep it that way, for however long it would last.

The service turned out to be really great that Sunday. This week we sang "Spirit Fall Down" by Luther Barnes and "Emmanuel" by Norman Hutchins. When offering time came, I could see Matthew watching as closely as he could. I hoped it was all a mistake and everything was back to normal. After service, a bunch of the church members decided to go out to Red Lobster for dinner even though I was totally against it. The babies didn't seem to like seafood lately, but I was willing to try and see what would happen. All the while hoping that it wasn't the worst. Lord knows I didn't want to spend the rest of the night throwing up or sick. If I did, I knew Matthew would be there to take care of me.

Dinner that night ended up being really nice. It was nice talking and fellowshipping with some of the saints and just having a great time. Everyone seemed to be so happy for us and were equally excited to meet the babies as well. All the mothers who were there told us stories about giving birth and what life is like after the babies come. They gave us some tips with the babies and also relationship advice, as they said it changes a bit after children. The biggest thing they kept telling us was to always try to find time for just us. It would get a little easier as the children got older and more independent, but not to let that get in the way of our relationship. Even though we had children, we still needed to find time for ourselves and our relationship. They also told us stories about their pregnancies, and I shared a few of my own that have happened thus far. We all enjoyed each other's company. There was a lot of laughter and good spirits.

It ended up being a fairly late night and we didn't get home till around ten o'clock. By this time, I was drained. I couldn't wait to get into the bed and go to sleep. But before I did, I wanted to ask Matthew about the offering today, and if he found any leads or what was going on.

"Did the offering come up short today?" I asked him.

"Sure did. It's really starting to get to me." He replied back. His face quickly frowned up.

"I have just one question. How exactly do you know that the offering is coming up short and whatnot?"

"Well, it's just simple logic and math. I know what the average offering normally is and it's a range. And when the pan comes up one and two hundred dollars short, it's hard not to know that something is wrong. There's also been a few times the amount in the envelope was different than what was written on the envelope, by a lot. Either that or everyone is going broke. I'm not really sure what is going on."

He tried to make light of the situation, but I knew he was only trying to make himself feel better.

"I see. What are you going to do?"

"I'm not sure. Maybe we can't pass the offering pan around anymore. Will just have to have everyone get up and walk to the front. It's just that it could take a longer amount of time. Maybe you guys could play some type of marching offering song or something. Or once the offering is done, they give the pan to you or Deacon Jones and either of you put it away. So, no one else is touching it before it gets to me."

"I agree. I'm sure you'll figure out something. I'm really tired so I'm going to sleep. Goodnight. I love you."

"I love you too cakes."

—

After Mariah fell asleep, I got up and went downstairs to my office. I couldn't fall asleep to save my life. I was still really bothered that the offering was coming up so short. This has been going on for about three weeks now, which is what makes it odd. One week, it'll be normal and then the next it'll hardly be anything in there. I did take into consideration that maybe people have fallen on hard times, but for it to just be for two weeks seems off. Maybe I'm overthinking it and nothing is going on. I don't want to bring it up to the congregation in fear they may think I'm just looking for money, because that's not the case. But I also don't want it to be the case that someone is indeed stealing. I'm going to pray about it, there's not much I can do right now. I'll rub Mariah's stomach till I fall asleep.

Chapter 22:

Move Over

It was now Wednesday, and Matthew and I were going to go to Baby Yoga. Now that I was about 22 weeks pregnant, we thought it would be a good idea to try the class out and see what the instructor had to say. We were both pretty excited about going. I was sure I was more excited than he was, but I was glad he agreed to come and be a part of this.

When we arrived at the center, we were greeted and asked to check in. After that we were shown the room where the class would be held. They had different level classes depending on how far along you were in your pregnancy and how many children you already had. That day, we were put in the class that had a mixture of both first- and second-time parents. When we walked into the room, everyone seemed to be greeting one another, so we joined in also. Matthew breathed a sigh of relief when he saw some other men in the room. I knew he was still a little on edge because he didn't want to be the only man there, but almost every woman that was there brought their partners.

I was a little nervous being there, but I stepped out of my comfort zone to introduce myself to a few of the mothers who were waiting in the room. I found out a few of them were almost ready to give birth, while others were still early in their pregnancies. For some of them, it was their second or third baby. One mother told me she was on baby number five and had been coming to baby yoga for all five pregnancies. She let me know all the instructors she had were amazing and that she thought I'd really enjoy the class. I asked her if all five pregnancies were planned or not. She told me her husband had a really good job that required him to travel a lot. They decided a while ago that she'd be a stay-at-home mom while he worked. The five children just happened to be a part of the deal. We both laughed and I told her congratulations. I truly believed children were a blessing, no matter how many you have.

Soon the class began, and we were each asked to introduce ourselves again to the class and the instructor. It was a small class, so it didn't take very long. Once it came my turn, I introduced Matthew and I, told them how far along I was in my pregnancy, and what we were having. I was the only one in the class having twins which was sort of cool. After the introduction ended, the instructor told us a little bit about herself and revealed that she too was pregnant. She also told us that she was a midwife and knew a lot about natural birth and different techniques to help make labor easier. Everything she would show us would be things that she's used during her own labor that worked. Hearing her stories made me less nervous about giving birth, I was so excited we decided to come.

We started off with a few stretches to warm our bodies up before jumping into anything else. The stretches she showed us allowed us to feel our bodies and open us up. It's easy to get tense and tight during your pregnancy and there's only so much stretching you can do. The instructor told us we could do these every day, multiple times a day if we needed to. I would be sure to include those in my night routine. After those, she led us in some breathing exercises and told us how to use them during labor and when having contractions. It was nothing like I saw on TV, where they do those short quick breaths. They were deep long breaths that were meant to keep you calm. She said that most women try to run from the pain when they should really embrace it. Your body knows what it's doing, and you need to trust that it knows.

Soon after that, it was time for the husbands to get to work. She showed them how they can be involved during the labor and how they can make it a bit easier on the women. She gave the men exercises to do with us while we were having contractions and different positions they could help us into to ease the pain as well. She also started giving the men exercises they could do at home to help the mothers out. Matthew really seemed to be enjoying himself the whole time the instructor worked with the men. I knew it would make him happy because he would be able to feel closer to the babies while doing all these types of exercises.

After she finished giving the men their exercises on how to help, the hour and a half was up. She led us in some "cool downs" as she called them before everyone went home. She let us know that every class she would give us different exercises to help with labor and breathing. Most of the women in the class were at least halfway through their pregnancies, so all the exercises she gave us would really come in handy soon. It would be cool to learn and do different types of things every week. We both enjoyed ourselves at the class and looked forward to next week.

When we returned home, it was still early in the evening and I decided that I would make dinner. I made a Korean dish with fish, rice, and vegetables. It had been a few days since I made dinner and Matthew seemed to really enjoy it. Even somewhat better than Chinese food. I had to explain to him that they are very similar, but it's the small things that make them very different. All in all, he ate plenty of it which was nice to see. I liked to see him eat my food, I guess it told me that I was doing a good job. After we finished eating, Matthew cleaned the kitchen while I got ready for bed. I always like to prepare for the next day before bed, but even more Wednesday nights than others. Thursdays were also so busy, dealing with work, church, and rehearsal. This way, I felt like I was getting a head start on the day.

Once he finished cleaning, he got ready for bed, while I was laying down. Shortly after, I started feeling the babies moving. I think that may have been their way of telling me they enjoyed the food as well. It was such an amazing feeling to feel them move, it felt like little taps inside my stomach. I had to pause and take in that moment because it was just that amazing. I could barely contain my excitement. I instantly called Matthew as I knew he would enjoy this just as much. When he came to the other side of the bed where I was laying, I told him to give me his hand and I placed it on my stomach. When he felt them, he jumped and then came the biggest smile I've ever seen from him. It's hard to explain the feeling I felt seeing him laughing and grinning like that. He laid down next to me and started talking to the babies and rubbing my stomach. It was so soothing, I ended up falling asleep. Matthew slept with his hand on my stomach all night just waiting for the babies to move again, he stayed like that most of the night.

—

Chapter 23:

Simple Things

I woke up the next morning feeling tired and a little sore. The instructor let the mothers know we might be sore after the class depending on how active we were in our pregnancies. Besides our nightly walks, I wasn't very active which probably wasn't the best idea. I hadn't really stretched much since I got pregnant, so I guess what we did in the class yesterday worked. I certainly didn't want to get out of bed, let alone go to work. But after calling Claire, I realized I had to because we had a meeting with a potential client. It was a business corporation that was being sued for miscommunication in a contract. The meeting was to discuss the claim and their needs. I was willing to take them on as a client, ensuring I'd be able to meet all of their requests. Since that was our only big meeting I decided to work from home after the meeting and rest.

I got to work around seven-fifty, about ten minutes before the meeting was to begin. That would be enough time to get everything I needed before heading to the conference room. The meeting lasted much longer than I expected; and by this time, it was almost ten-thirty. Since the meeting was the only reason for coming to work, I figured I'd go home to take a nap. I couldn't wait to get home and eat. Anything else I had to do had to wait until after my nap. When I returned home, I found Matthew and Daniel talking in the living room. Matthew told me when I left, he'd be working from home because he had some church stuff to work on as well. I was hoping that maybe he figured out the whole money situation and I also hoped that he didn't want me to know about it. At least not right now because I was tired. I figured I'd say hi and make my way upstairs.

"Hey guys", I said, walking in and kissing Matthew.

"Hey", they both replied.

Matthew looked so preoccupied that he barely looked up when I came to kiss him.

"Babe, I'm going to go lay down for a bit."

"Ok, I'll be up in a little while." He replied.

I was hoping that wasn't for a chat.

After I woke from my nap, I went downstairs to find Matthew in his office doing some work. Now that I was rested and feeling better, I wanted to know what was happening earlier.

"Hey baby. So, what was Daniel doing here earlier? Is everything okay?" I asked.

"Yes, everything is fine. We were just talking about changing the way that we do the offering like we talked about before." He replied.

"Oh, what did he say?"

"He thought it would be a good idea, anything to stop what's going on. He also thought he may have a lead to what is going on."

"Really? He knows who is doing it?"

"Kind of… Daniel said that he overheard a conversation between two deacons last Sunday. He didn't intend to eavesdrop but what they were talking about caught his ear. One of the deacons mentioned how he had been short on money. Whoever he was talking to asked him what he was going to do, and he said he had a plan, but someone wouldn't like it. Daniel didn't know who that someone was, but that deacon also happens to lift and count the offerings."

My mouth instantly dropped, I knew the deacon he was referring to and I couldn't believe he'd do something like that. Steal from the church? To me that was going a little too far. Deacon Patterson was always so nice and kind, he always volunteered to help with church events and activities, I always thought of him as being so giving. He'd been going to the church for about three and a half years. He and his wife moved from San Francisco to Downtown LA, which was closer to the church. He was a deacon at the church they previously attended, and after they became members, he told Matthew that he'd like to continue being a deacon at GPC if that was okay. Of course, Matthew agreed since he needed the help. That was around the time he was starting to move into the new building. If anyone knew how giving Matthew was, it would be any of the church staff as they knew him the best. I was still in shock from hearing this.

"Wow, are you serious? You think it may have been Deacon Patterson?"

"Well, I didn't want to call any names out, but yes. That's who Daniel overheard talking."

"Do you really think he would steal like that? I mean, he's been a big help to the church and he's always volunteered to help you no matter what it is."

"You never know what people will do when they are down. I would hope he wouldn't do anything like this but what does, "someone may not like it mean"? Someone like who? Me… his wife?"

"But all he had to do was ask, you would've given him whatever he needed."

"You're right, I would have but what does the bible say about being prideful? In his pride, the wicked man does not seek him; in all his thoughts there is no room for God."

"Psalm 10:4." I replied.

"Exactly, humble yourself, therefore, under the mighty hand of God so that at the proper time he will exalt you. He wasn't thinking about anyone but himself. What's the point of sewing into a church you can't go to and ask for help?"

"So, what are you guys going to do now with the offering? Are you going to confront him?"

"Well, Daniel and Deacon Jones will be in charge of handling the money. We'll have everyone walk up instead of passing the plate around. Either Daniel or Deacon Jones will give the money to you in an envelope and you can count it. thought about it, but I don't have any real proof that it is him. So, I'm not going to confront him. I'll get my answer if the offerings start being regular again after this. I'm going to tell him that we wanted to try a new way to do the offering now, and no longer need his assistance with the money; he can help in other ways. I never questioned his past or even what happened at the church they were at previously. We don't know the real reason why they left."

"Well then, it's settled. I'll talk to Carl about coming up with some type of fly song to play during the offering."

"Fly?" he said laughing. "That'll work, but enough about that. How are you feeling?"

"I feel a little better. I'm still a little queasy but I feel rested, that nap really helped, I am hungry though. Did you make anything to eat?"

"Umm, I thought you were going to handle that. I was waiting for you to get up."

"Really Matthew?" I said angrily, "I've been sick."

"Naw, I'm just messing; I made some Italian Pizza. I know you weren't feeling well. I made sure I handled lunch and I made enough for dinner. I wouldn't do that to you."

"I can't believe you." I said, rolling my eyes.

I really thought after the way I looked when I walked in, he was going to make me cook dinner. If it were up to me, I would've made sandwiches or ordered something. I guess he was getting me back for all the times I joked with him. We finished our conversation, then headed upstairs to eat. It was about two-thirty in the afternoon, a little late for lunch but either way I was starving. I sat down and Matthew made me a plate. I was so glad that Matthew knew how to cook well. Because honestly, I wouldn't know what to do. We couldn't possibly eat out every night and some nights I didn't feel like getting up, let alone cooking a meal, and my husband can eat.

The pizza turned out to be really good. He made the dough from scratch, as well as the sauce. He put mozzarella and parmesan cheese, Italian sausage, and some different types of herbs and spices. It tasted better than any store-bought pizza out there. It was a good thing he made a big pizza, because I must've eaten almost half of it, I was so hungry. It got the babies kicking and moving around and Matthew was excited to feel them. After we ate, I took my spot on the couch to put my feet up and do some work. We had rehearsal and bible study tonight and I wanted to get some work done before we left.

Time flew as we sat on the couch and finished working. By the time I was finished answering all the emails I had and edited two briefs, it was already four-fifteen and we needed to head to the church. Rehearsal didn't start until five, but Matthew liked to get there early. When we pulled into the parking lot, no one was there yet. I went to get the organ warmed up before everyone started pouring in. About 30 minutes later, Deacon Patterson walked in the church and greeted everyone. He would sometimes come early to help straighten up the church and take out the trash. I couldn't help but think about Matthew and I's conversation from earlier. Matthew came out of his office and asked Deacon Patterson to speak with him, I figured he would tell him about changing the offering. I couldn't stick around because it was time for rehearsal to start.

—

I was still upset and slightly disappointed thinking about my conversation with Daniel and Mariah earlier. Deacon Patterson was always so willing to help around the church. He and Deacon Jones were two of my favorite saints because I knew no matter what, they would go out of their way to help. It saddens me to think Deacon Patterson would do something so cold-blooded and steal from the church. I would have given my last, even from my own pocket to help him if I needed to. I didn't want him to think anything was up since we were changing the offering, so I figured I'd speak with him before church Sunday. I didn't want there to be any surprises or catch him off guard. I knew he usually arrived at the church early on Thursdays to straighten up, so I decided to speak to him then. I pulled him into my office and broke the ice to ensure things wouldn't be tense. I told him the news and he immediately said okay and asked why. I didn't want him to know the offerings were short, as only Daniel, Deacon Jones, Mariah, and I knew. I let him know I wanted to try something different and make sure the congregation feels engaged in the service. I also thought that would be a good way for them to stretch from sitting down before the word came. He agreed and we continued to chat for a little before he went to his normal chores. He took the news well and even agreed with the change. I was hoping this change would prove me wrong but only time would tell.

—

I couldn't wait to get in the car to ask Matthew what happened with Deacon Patterson, I hoped everything went well or as well as it could.

"How did it go?" I asked him, as we drove home.

"Well, I think it went well. I told him we'd be changing the way we do offering, and he asked why. I told him I just wanted to try things differently and give the saints a chance to get up and move. He agreed and we started talking about our lives and the babies."

"So, he seemed to take it okay?"

"It appears so. I told him I would need his help in other areas of the church, such as with cleaning and perhaps equipment setup. He could get with Tim to see what he would need."

"Okay, good. I'm glad everything is okay."

"Me too. I hope this proves me wrong about him."

"And if it doesn't?"

"I did my part, I'll let God handle the rest."
We continued our ride home, stopping at the grocery store on the way. I told him the babies wanted some ice cream. Any time I say the babies want something, he asks no questions and gets it. When we got home, I had another piece of pizza with some ice cream to follow. We took showers and laid down together. The babies were moving a lot now since that first night. And once again, Matthew took his spot next to my stomach.

It makes me so happy to see him enjoying himself with the babies. It's easy for me to talk and bond with them because they are always with me. But I know that he has to do a little extra to be closer with them. I love when we are about to go to bed because he always rubs my feet; then lies on my stomach and rubs it while talking to the babies. He tells them everything like who he is and how he can't wait for them to get here. He says he wants to make sure they know their father's voice. I tell him that they will know, but he wants to make sure he says. He tells them they're already beautiful even though he hasn't seen them. He says, "I just know." He even tells them about his day and what he did; It's so cute. Usually by the time he finishes, I am either half asleep or fully asleep. Surprisingly, it's pretty soothing.

The next morning came and Matthew and I decided to take the day off. We literally stayed in bed all day talking, listening to music, and occasionally watching a little television. He made us breakfast and lunch, and for dinner we ordered takeout. Something I hadn't had in such a long time, Chili's. It's something common but it was so good. These days, the simplest meals taste so good to me. The day was so relaxing and calming. I didn't have to worry about work and Matthew wasn't concerned with anything from work or from the church. The feeling took me back to our honeymoon with no worries or cares. It felt good to get away mentally seeing that we'd both been so busy since we got back. Between the wedding, buying and moving into the house, the pregnancy, work, all while adjusting to being married, we were struggling to find time for each other and ourselves. It really was nice just lying with my husband not having a care in the world. Just me… and Matthew.

Chapter 24:

The Baby Shower

I was getting to the end of my pregnancy and frankly, I couldn't wait to have these babies. I had about another month and a half to go, give or take a few weeks. The doctor mentioned that twins usually don't go full term and we'd probably have to induce within the next few weeks if they didn't come on their own. My belly was huge and super tight, and the babies were running out of space. I was getting to that point where I couldn't sleep as much, and the babies were constantly moving around with nowhere to go. We were on opposite sleep schedules. When I wanted to sleep, they were awake and vice versa. I even had to start taking time off from work because I couldn't sleep at night.

It was now time for the baby shower, and I was so excited. I was in the dark about the whole thing, since Jhana wanted to make it a total surprise. When she asked me if she could plan the baby shower I thought why not? It would be less stress on my part, as I was already busy, but I hated not knowing what was going on. Jhana called me one day and asked me to give her a list of names of who I wanted to be there, both men and women. I gave her the list, and I've heard nothing about it since. Even though I knew it was in good hands, I still wanted to know what was going on and what she planned. She told us the time and place and I told her I'd be there.

When Matthew and I arrived at the venue, we were greeted by the hotel bellhop and staff. Jhana decided to have the baby shower at the Hyatt ballroom where Matthew and I had our wedding reception. We walked in, hand in hand and everyone shouted, "Surprise". And it truly was, everything was so beautiful, and it was so nice to see everyone again. She invited both our parents, lots of friends and loved ones. There were even people there from the church. I couldn't help but cry as I was overjoyed with happiness. Jhana really outdid herself with everything. She had decorations, pictures of me and Matthew up all around, and even pictures from my maternity shoot. She had some of the hotel staff there to serve and greet everyone who walked in. I was extremely shocked at all the detail she put into everything. It was such a nice atmosphere.

Matthew and I were ushered over to our seats at a table facing all the other tables in the front. We greeted some friends and family members on our way to our seats; it was so hard to contain all my excitement. Everyone was so happy for us and excited to see me as well. As soon as we sat down, Jhana grabbed the microphone and began to proceed with the program. She really planned this whole thing out, "Now that our guests of honor have arrived, we can proceed. First, we are going to have a few words of encouragement from friends and family. Try to keep it short and sweet as there are a lot of people who would like to speak. After that, lunch will be served." Jhana said. The first to speak was my brother Cameron, he had everyone laughing telling stories of when we were kids and how happy he was for me. Leave it to my siblings to share the embarrassing moments of when we were kids and how he thought I'd be with my own children.

Next were our parents, they had great advice for Matthew and I after the babies came. They told us how important it would be for us to support each other and that would be the time we'd need it the most. My mom also told us to take some time for ourselves before the babies come. Once they were here, it was going to be hard to get away for the first few months. Everyone agreed that life was going to get very busy very fast. I was sure I wanted both my mom and Matthew's mom to be there for the birth. I was extremely nervous and wanted all the support I could get. Once the mothers finished speaking, Matthew's father gave us some words of encouragement as well.

"We never thought our son would be the first to get married from the bunch, but we sure are proud of who he married. Even before we met Mariah, we knew that she was the one for him. Every time we spoke to him on the phone, all he ever talked about was her. We instantly started praying for you guys. I'm so glad to be having our very first grandchildren and who would have thought they'd get twins on the first try! Either way, I'm excited. We will help any way that we can. I guess to sum everything up, we are proud of you both and can't wait to be grandparents."

With his words came tears, it felt so great having in-laws that were sweet and most of all they accepted me. After they spoke, some other friends and family spoke as well. So, many people had such great words for us and gave us many congratulations and blessings. I saw so many friends and cousins that couldn't make it to the wedding as well. The room was filled with love and you could feel it.

After the encouraging words, Jhana told the waiters to bring out lunch. The hotel catered the meal, and it was great! We had potatoes and gravy, lots of different vegetables such as broccoli, corn, and salad;

baked chicken, fish, rice, and some other finger foods. I think it's safe to say I ate way too much. I was ready to take a nap after eating, but I was sure the excitement of everything would keep me awake.

Once lunch was over, it was time for games. We played a game similar to musical chairs but Jhana called it, "Pass the Baby", where everyone stands in a circle, a song is played and it simultaneously stops. Whoever has the baby when the song stops loses and leaves the circle. You keep playing until there's only one person standing and the winner receives a prize. We played about three rounds of the game, as it went quickly and everyone seemed to enjoy it. Cameron was a great DJ, making the game more fun by stopping the music back-to-back. It got to the point where people were almost throwing the baby to prevent the music from stopping on them. The game was a big hit. The next game we played was called, "Choose the Name". This is where everyone chooses two names they think we should name the twins. We found out that we were having twin girls which made the game easier. This would definitely help us with naming them because that was one thing that I hadn't thought of yet. We played a few more games that Jhana came up with before moving to the next activity. She kept everyone busy and there wasn't much downtime which was nice.

After all the fun and games, it was time to open the gifts we received. This was my favorite part of the whole day, other than seeing everyone. We got so many good gifts like baby clothes, bottles and pacifiers, baby formula, bibs, and two bottle warmers which would really come in handy. They were designed to heat the bottles to the exact temperature to where it wouldn't burn the baby, and it only took a matter of seconds. I figured we'd keep one upstairs and one downstairs because why not. It would save time and the effort of having to go downstairs often. We also got two cribs from my parents and two car seats and a stroller from Matthew's parents. We were both so ecstatic with what we received. This meant we wouldn't have to buy much. At least for the first few months.

After opening the gifts, we ate cupcakes and proceeded to wrap everything up.

"Wow. I first just want to thank everyone for coming out and celebrating this joyous occasion with us. It feels so great to be loved by family and friends like yourselves and we are truly honored. We thank you all for the gifts that we received and all the fun we had today. I want to especially thank my awesome sister Jhana for planning all this. It literally wouldn't have happened if it wasn't for her. I couldn't be more grateful. Everything was beautiful and perfect and it was a pleasant surprise." I said to everyone before we finally ended the shower.

They clapped and after more hugs and congratulations, they all made their way to the door. We said our goodbyes to everyone and thanked them once again for coming. It was now around six o'clock and I was tired. Most of our family members weren't heading back home until tomorrow, so some of them came back to our house to relax before calling it a night. Jhana and our parents would stay the night with us. When Matthew and I got home, we decided to put everything in one of the guest rooms because the painters were coming tomorrow to finish painting the baby's rooms. I was actually glad they were staying with us because we had so much stuff to take inside. It was hard to believe the babies would be here in less than two months. Time seemed to go by so fast. Once the baby's rooms were finished, we'd put all the furniture in them and then wait for them to get here. We decided that it would make sense to just use one room for now, seeing as they would be together most of the time anyways, and it would be easier for me and Matthew.

After everyone loaded everything in the house, we all sat downstairs to catch up.

"So, tell us, how has everything been?" Matthew's dad jumped right into the conversation, as we sat down.

"Well, honestly, it's been a little busy getting everything together. But we've gotten the house stuff taken care of. I believe we're handling things well. I replied to his dad.

"How has the adjustment been from being married to now having babies?" Matthew's mother asked. They wanted to know everything.

"A shock." Matthew replied while laughing.

Everyone paused and laughed for a little.

"It's been exciting to say the least. I feel like we were just about to get into a groove of things, and then Mariah found out she was pregnant. So now our focus has switched to the babies." Matthew continued.

"But don't forget what we told you.", my mom started. We all paused because I couldn't remember what she told us.

"What is that"? I asked.

"Continue making time for each other and your relationship. Don't get so consumed with the children that you forget about yourselves. You are just as important, if not more, than your children. One day, they will leave you, so you can't be so consumed with them. Of course, be great parents and love them. But still continue to date and find time for you. Even now." My mom always seemed to know the right things to say.

"Yes, I agree with that. That is something your father struggled with once I became a stay-at-home mom. Our relationship took a toll for a while because I was so consumed with the needs of the children and the house, I forgot about his needs too. One day your father hired a babysitter, something I would have never done, just so we could get out of the house and go on a date. I didn't realize how much I missed just us until that moment. Don't wait too late like we did to realize you still need each other." His mother added on.

I hadn't really thought about our relationship after kids. I figured everything would keep moving as it has, but what they said made a lot of sense. I wanted our marriage to prosper, especially since we had children so early on. I knew I was willing to make whatever sacrifices and choices to continue dating and working on our marriage even with children. I never wanted to lose us.

"Wow, that's great advice. I know I will keep that in mind throughout everything." Matthew replied.

"I agree." I replied smiling at Matthew.

"Do you guys have a lot more to do before the babies come?" My dad asked us.

"Not too much more. Matthew said we could hire an interior designer to design their rooms, the same one who did our house actually. So, they've been doing the majority of work with the rooms. We picked out the color schemes and designs and she started bringing it to life."

"Interior designer huh?" My dad laughed.

My dad was simple, so I was sure he didn't understand the hype of everything we were doing.

"Yes dad." I laughed. "She did really great designing the house, so we decided to bring her back.

"What's the color schemes and design ideas?" Matthew's mom asked.

"One room will be pink and yellow and the other pink and purple. We're going to paint their names on the walls, Matthew's idea. We also choose furniture to place in the rooms and she'll place everything where it should do. I'll wash all their clothes and blankets once it's all set up. Once the rooms are done, we'll be ready for them to come."

"Seems like y'all have it all together." My mom said.

We did and we were super excited for them to get here. We chatted a little while longer before I headed upstairs. It was past my bedtime and I was starting to feel it.

As I laid down, I reflected on the day. I have such a great sister for putting this all together and amazing parents and in-laws for all their help. I knew my babies would be loved and I wouldn't have to worry about anything.

Chapter 25:

Reminisce

It seems as though time is going by so fast. It was almost two years ago, I was a typical girl who had just graduated from law school and scored a dream job. I met an awesome best friend at a café who introduced me to my now husband. What more could I ask for? My life has changed so much in just a short amount of time and in less than a month, two baby girls will be here. I often take a step back and take everything in, because I don't want to forget just how blessed I am. It's like God had taken the time out of his day to recognize a little girl from Denver who had big dreams and decided to honor them. For that I am grateful. Matthew is the guy of my dreams and has been so amazing over this last year of us dating, and then getting married. If anyone asked me two years ago my goals for the next few years, I'm not sure if a wedding and babies would have made that list. Getting married was definitely in my plan, but I never imagined it happening so soon. It's good to look back at the blessings I was so lucky to receive.

It was now Tuesday, about two weeks since the baby shower. This would be my last doctor's appointment before they would be inducing me. Since the baby shower, the babies grew a lot, and it was getting really tight for them inside my stomach. I still had about four and a half weeks left but the doctor mentioned it was unsafe for them to remain inside. I was both nervous and excited for this. Excited because the babies would finally be here, but nervous because they were coming soon. Today would be the day we'd schedule the induction with the doctor and talk about the process. Matthew seemed to be full of excitement, but that was understandable because he wasn't the one that had to go through labor. I wanted everything to go as smoothly as possible and I wanted the babies to be as healthy as they could be, especially with them being twins.

When we arrived at the doctor's office, we did our normal check-in and proceeded to the room. First, the doctor checked the baby's heart beats, and we were able to see them one last time while they were still inside my stomach. She also checked to see if I had dilated, which I hadn't. She told us about the process and what would happen when it was time to induce. She also talked a little about labor, which nothing could prepare me for. After she poured all types of information out to us, she asked if we had any questions before going on our way. I was so nervous I could barely think straight, I was sure I had questions, I just couldn't think of what they were. She let us know we could call her or the nurse if anything came up before the induction. We scheduled the induction for next Tuesday morning at 8:00am. I had just about a week until I could meet my girls.

Since the induction was a week away, our parents decided to extend their stay to help us with the babies. Originally, they planned to fly back home after the baby shower to return in a few weeks for their arrival, but no sense in returning now. They were coming sooner than we all expected. There was still a lot to do after the baby shower and our parents said they needed a vacation. Their vacation ended up being longer than they expected but I was thankful to have them here with us. I knew having my mother there by my side would help me through the process. After leaving the doctor's office, we went back home, and I took my mother out to lunch. I filled them in on what the doctor told us about the induction and that it was scheduled for next week.

"Wow, you're so big! Those babies are really growing. How was the appointment?" my mom said with excitement. She always made it a point to let me know how big I was every time she saw me.

"I know, I really am and everything is going well. I have no complaints. They scheduled the induction for next Tuesday. The doctor said the babies are getting big and quickly running out of room to grow. On top of that, literally everything hurts, sometimes it hurts to breathe. Lately, I haven't wanted to leave the bed, let alone the house." I replied.

"I know how I felt being pregnant, but I can't imagine how you're feeling with two babies inside you." she answered.

"I feel very, very heavy." I laughed back.

"Well, Tuesday is soon. Are you nervous?" she asked.

"Yes, I am very nervous, but also very excited. I've heard a lot of labor and delivery stories, but I know everyone's labor is different, so I'm not sure what to expect. I just pray everything goes smoothly and the babies aren't extremely small. The doctor told us they'll most likely be premature, but that can vary as well."

"You have a lot of people praying for you and those babies. I have faith they will be as healthy as they should be, and your labor will be fine."

"Thanks mom. You always know what to say."

We continued talking as we ate, and she gave me more advice about labor. I must admit, I was a bit scared, but one thing the yoga instructor kept saying during the classes was to remain calm and let your body do the work. She reminded all the women to trust yourself and continue thinking positive thoughts. I had to keep telling myself that I can do this. After we finished lunch, we went back home to relax. I was ready to put my feet up after a busy afternoon. Our new home had so much room, both our parents planned to stay with us, rather than paying for a hotel. This way they could help us with the babies and whatever else we needed. I hoped it wouldn't be too much having them there, but then again, I wasn't sure how Matthew and I would do all of this by ourselves. At least in the beginning. The baby's rooms were now finished and furnished. My mom and Matthew's mom started helping me put all of their clothes away and getting the hospital bags together. My mom was happy to be included in whatever aspect she could. I couldn't help but remember the times when I was younger doing things with my mom. Now I am grown, and about to start making memories with my own children. We spent the rest of the day talking, folding clothes, and enjoying our time together.

Chapter 26:

The Birth

Sunday morning rolled around too quickly and that meant it was time for church. I wasn't feeling up to it at all. I didn't get much sleep last night and I was in a lot of pain. Since my dad was an OB/GYN, he thought maybe I was going to go into labor soon which freaked me out. Twins don't usually go full term, so I knew he was telling the truth. I was also a few days away from my induction date, which also put me on edge. Matthew and I had been up since about six o'clock that morning dealing with pain and contractions. Around seven he went to shower and get dressed for church. Since I was up most of the night having contractions, I told him I was going to stay home and try to get some rest. He looked so exhausted, but I knew he didn't want to miss service since he was preaching today. The contractions were somewhat strong, but they weren't frequent enough to go to the hospital.

Matthew left around nine, a little earlier than normal, so I thought I'd try to get some sleep, which didn't happen. The babies were moving around, and I felt so much pressure on my lower abdomen. My mom did her best to comfort me, but nothing seemed to work. I was extremely tired after being up half the night and it didn't seem like I'd be able to sleep anytime soon. Maybe my dad was right about the babies coming soon. Anything would be better than this at this point. I was in such an uncomfortable position. About an hour after Matthew left, I started having contractions more frequently and these things are no joke. They started to come about every ten minutes or so for the next two hours and then my water broke. I didn't know whether to sit there or to get up, so I just yelled for my mom. She ran upstairs to see what was wrong and I told her that my water had just broken. She got so excited and ran downstairs to tell my dad and Matthew's mom. My dad rushed upstairs to see if I was okay and helped me downstairs. I changed my clothes and made my way to the car. My mom grabbed my bag and we all piled in the car and headed to the hospital. Today is the big day.

I sat in the back seat with Matthew's parents, while my mom drove and my dad sat in the passenger seat, trying to get in contact with Matthew. He needed to meet us at the hospital, but I was worried since he was in service that we wouldn't be able to get in contact with him. I knew that he wouldn't answer his phone because he was in service, but my dad tried anyway. When he didn't answer, I started to get agitated because I didn't want him to miss the birth. The contractions were getting more intense and I could feel the babies shifting. I needed him to be there with me. My mom asked if there was anyone else they could call that could relay the message. I remembered Krystal or Daniel should be at church and that they'd probably answer. My dad tried calling Daniel first, and after multiple tries, he finally picked up his phone.

"Hello", Daniel answered.

"Hi Daniel, this is Mariah's dad Bryce. I'm calling to get in touch with Matthew. Mariah's water broke and we are on our way to the hospital. Can you tell him to meet us there please?" My dad said.

"Oh, goodness, that's exciting! I'll tell him right now." Daniel replied.

"Thank you so much."

"You're welcome."

I was relieved now that Matthew knew what was happening, we were soon to be united.

The ride to the hospital seemed like forever but we finally got there. The hospital was about 30 minutes away and I had contractions the entire time. Thankfully, traffic wasn't too bad but all the bumps in the road made the pain worse. We had barely gotten things started and I was already over labor. I wanted the babies to be here already. When we arrived at the hospital, my mom pulled up to the front doors so my dad could get me a wheelchair. He helped me out of the car and rolled me inside, while the valet parked the car. My mom checked me in while the nurses rolled me to get settled in the room. Matthew arrived at the hospital about 10 minutes after we did. The nurses were still hooking me up to the monitors and everything. He rushed in, kissed me, and right then I knew that I was going to be ok. Once the nurses finished prepping me, it was time for the waiting game. My contractions were still coming about every ten minutes and the doctors told us that we had a while to go. I was only about three centimeters dilated, which wasn't the best news. But since my water had already broken, hopefully the labor would progress enough, and I could push soon. Matthew stayed by the bed and held my hand.

About three hours had passed and I was now five centimeters dilated. But still not enough to start pushing. To my surprise, the pain of the contractions seemed to calm down a bit. I was even able to get some rest in between contractions every now and then. It was now about three o'clock in the afternoon and we had been here since about eleven.

Matthew was laid out in one of the recliner chairs, our moms and Matthew's dad were talking, and my dad seemed to be resting as well. Every so often a contraction would come, and I would feel like I was going to die and then it would subside.

After Matthew got some rest, he got up and talked with me for a while. It was calming and it kept my mind off the pain for a little. The room they put me in was a good size, so everyone could relax comfortably. Shortly after Matthew woke up, my dad got up and asked if there were any updates. I told him the nurses came and checked on me about thirty minutes ago and there wasn't much progress. I could tell he was starting to get antsy and impatient. That's when he started to pace back and forth in front of the bed. I knew he was excited to meet the babies, but he seemed more nervous than I was. He was starting to get on my nerves, so I told him to go wait in the lobby. He didn't want to go nor did he want to sit down but I couldn't take the pacing back and forth. Matthew's dad went out there with him to keep him company. Hopefully it wouldn't be too much longer, we were all starting to get impatient.

About an hour and a half later, the doctor came back into the room and checked me once more. In the last two hours, I had dilated three more centimeters. There was only about two more centimeters to go and I could start pushing. I was so ready to get these babies out of me. As the labor progressed and I dilated more, I began to get more and more uncomfortable. The contractions picked up once again and they were stronger than before. Doc encouraged me to try laying on my side and walking around a little to ease the pain. Laying on my side didn't really help but I did walk around the room which did help. My mom let us all know my dad was still pacing in the waiting area. I wanted the babies to come soon for his sake.

Another hour had passed, and I was finally nine centimeters, which meant I was ready to start pushing. The pressure was so intense, it felt like they were going to come out on their own without me pushing. Even though my body was ready, I didn't know if I was mentally ready. At this point it was now or...now. Doc called for the nurses and they soon came flooding in to get everything set up. Since we were having twins, they had two teams. Team A to care for one baby and Team B to care for the other.

I was starting to get anxious and I felt my heart beating fast. My breathing picked up and I no longer seemed to be in control. I was shaking and suddenly I didn't trust my body any longer. Up until this point, I had been great. But now at the final moment, I wasn't sure I was prepared for what was about to happen. One of the nurses saw the worry on my face and came over to offer comforting words.

"Hey lady, what's going on? You've been cruising through this labor the entire day. Don't quit on me now! You're almost there. Take a few deep breaths and wait for the doctor to tell you to push. Just relax, this is the final stretch."

I got out of my head, took a few deep breaths while the nurses finished setting up and mentally prepared myself to meet my babies. I could see the excitement over Matthew's face, but he tried not to let it show much.

It took the nurses about 10 minutes to set everything up and get their scrubs and gloves on, but it felt much longer. I could feel the babies like right on the edge and it was hard not to push. It felt like I had to use the restroom, but I had to hold it in. Finally, the doctor came to do one final check, but there was no need. She could see one of their heads and it was time to assume the position to push. Matthew held my right hand, and his mother held my left, while my mother stood at the end of the bed to record the babies coming. I wanted to be able to watch the birth later. Both our dads were still in the waiting room, but my mother let them know I was getting ready to push and she would get them once it was over. My dad could finally stop pacing. Doctor Sanders told me to get ready and relax until I felt a contraction. Once the contraction came, I could push. Seconds after she said that I felt a strong contraction come on.

"Ok now, Push!" Doc said.

The countdown began.

"10, 9, 8, 7, 6, 5, 4, 3, 2, 1. Ok. Relax for a minute." She said.

So much ran through my head at that moment. I can't believe that I was about to push two babies out of me. I can't wait for them to be here and see their beautiful faces. I felt another contraction coming which meant it was time to push again. Doc started the countdown once more. In a matter of seconds, I heard crying and got so excited I started crying as well. Doc placed the first baby on my chest and I cradled her close to my heart. The second baby was still on her way down. When I looked into her eyes, an instant love connection formed. I never felt so much love for one person in my life. That moment could have lasted forever. Matthew cut her umbilical cord before the nurse came over and wrapped her in a blanket. Then the nurse handed her over to him because I still had some work to do. He cradled her head and smiled, it was the best feeling in the world. Her name would be Kamille Marie. Matthew and the nurse went over to the baby warmer to do all the necessary checks before the next baby came.

Ten minutes later, it was time for baby number two to come. The contractions didn't stop but the pressure eased up slightly, then got really intense again. I got ready to push and Doctor Sanders did the countdown. After about four pushes, Kaila Marin was born. Doctor Sanders placed her on my chest and the feeling I had before came flooding back again. They were both so beautiful and most of all they were healthy. The nurses let us know they were breathing on their own and they were a good weight as well. Our dads came back in the room and held them before they were taken to the NICU. Even though they were a good weight, they were still on the smaller side and Kaila had a little fluid in her lungs, so they had to be monitored to ensure they were okay. I hated that I wouldn't be able to hold them longer. They were a part of me, and I was in love. The nurses assured me as soon as they were cleared, they would bring them back to the room. Since they would be in the NICU, I figured I'd get some rest as well. I was so exhausted after the day's events. I still couldn't believe I was a mother now.

I spent most of that night sleeping, with the occasional checks from the nurses. After a few hours, they brought the babies back into the room for more skin to skin and to feed them. I had already planned to breastfeed ahead of time. Once the nurses brought them back, they were both placed on my chest to try and latch. Breastfeeding was a little more complicated than I expected it to be. Kamille didn't want to latch, leading me to believe she would be the stubborn one. When the doctor came back, she let me know it was normal for babies not to latch immediately and not to worry, we would keep trying throughout the night. Until they did, my mom advised me to pump and bottle feed what came out.

The next morning came and the twins were doing a lot better. Kaila's breathing was much clearer now and they weren't hearing any fluid in her lungs. Kamille decided she was hungry enough to latch on and I was able to feed them both. Latching seemed to be more efficient at helping my milk come in and the twins both seemed more satisfied than from the bottle. I decided to breastfeed them early in my pregnancy for as long as I could. I wanted to make sure they got all the vitamins and nutrients they could while they were babies. The lactation specialist also came and showed me all the ways to breastfeed, and the do's and don'ts while feeding them. I was still extremely tired from the night before, as I didn't sleep as much as I hoped. All the excitement from the babies kept me awake, but I was able to hold them and the nurses said they could stay in the room with us. They would continue to monitor them in case anything went wrong.

Over the course of the day, we had a lot of visitors come by. Krystal and Daniel came, then Claire came shortly after. Carl, his wife, and his daughter came by and brought lots of laughs. Carl couldn't believe Matthew was a dad and joked about how he'd have three women ruling his life. Matthew soaked it all up and told Carl he couldn't wait. After they left, Eden and Jhana stopped by. They were both so excited and gushed over the babies. They took turns holding them, saying how perfect they were. The last person to visit was Mother Massey. Matthew told her how great I did during the labor and that I did it all naturally. She hugged and kissed me and told me how proud of me she was. She also said that she was praying the entire time after she found out. She had faith everything would be smooth, and it was. Everyone brought gifts and lots of love and said how beautiful they were.

That day turned out to be rather demanding and I was beat by the time Mother Massey left. The doctor came in and let us know the babies were doing a little better than they all assumed. They wouldn't have to spend more than a few days at the hospital before we could take them home. Matthew and I steadily prayed they would gain weight and stayed healthy so we could take them home sooner. Since Kaila came second, she was the smallest out of the two, everyone was really worried about her. She had some trouble breathing at first, but it soon cleared up. The first night, they put her on a ventilator but by the next day she had recovered. One of the nurses said the ventilator and breastfeeding helped her a lot. She was breathing on her own, just not as strong as she should be. I couldn't wait to bring my babies home!

Chapter 27:

Am I Dreaming?

Friday is finally here, I am so excited! The hospital is discharging the twins and we can finally take them home. Even though it's only been a few days, it seemed so much longer, because I missed them. I stayed in the hospital with the twins for a few days before they released me. I didn't want to leave without taking them with me, but the doctor couldn't have me stay there if nothing was wrong. Matthew and I went back and forth between home and the hospital until they were strong enough to come home. I would pump at home and bring the milk to the hospital for the night and breastfeed them during the day. Thankfully, they only had to stay two more days after I left. They were both so strong throughout this whole process. I, on the other hand, had a hard time. Matthew and I spent most of those two days at the hospital, as long as they would let us. When the hospital called us, I ran to the door so quickly, I left Matthew behind, excitement was an understatement, I couldn't wait to bring my baby's home. When we walked into the NICU, they were all ready to be taken home. The nurses also gave us some goodies to take home with us.

When we finally arrived home, Matthew brought them upstairs to our room so I could feed them. Since I left the hospital, I had been pumping as much as I could those last few days. The lactation specialist informed me that pumping would be beneficial to ensure I had enough milk throughout their time breastfeeding. She mentioned it could be a lot trying to feed the twins at the same time, so having a bottle for someone else to feed them would be helpful. I had been pumping as much as I could while I was at the hospital with them and when I went home. I stored up a good amount of milk, but I knew it wouldn't last long because their appetites were starting to pick up. Breastfeeding was something I was extremely excited about. I recounted all the stories I heard about breastfeeding, the joys and pains. I am looking forward to all of it. I still can't wrap my mind around the fact I am now a mother of twins.

The first night with the twins turned out to be a sleepless one. They stayed up the entire night crying and I couldn't figure out what was wrong with them. Matthew's parents and my dad had flown home, but my mom stayed a little while longer. I'm so glad she decided to stay because she was such a big help. Somehow when she held them, they stopped crying and went straight to sleep. I couldn't figure out what she was doing, but I knew I had to figure something out before she left because we would eventually need some sleep. Once she put them to sleep, they stayed asleep for about two hours before waking up to eat again. After I fed them, they went back to sleep, and I was able to get some rest. Matthew had passed out a few hours before. So, it would be his turn when they woke up, momma was tired.

Friday came and went much quicker than I expected. It was Saturday morning, our second day with them and I didn't realize how much work two babies would be! I was prepared for the sleepless nights, but they came sooner than I expected. I was hoping they wouldn't last too long. My mother planned to stay with us until Tuesday and I was already sad thinking about life after she left. She cooked, cleaned, and helped us with the babies. I wasn't sure how we'd survive without her. I'll admit, the last few weeks I was spoiled.

Surprisingly, I was more nervous than I anticipated about actually being a mother to twins. Certainly, I knew it would be a lot of work, but now all my fears started to set in. I wanted to be the best mom I could be for them and it was hard not knowing what the future held. It's hard knowing if you're doing things the right way or what things will work for them. We had received so much advice throughout the pregnancy, it was hard to know where to begin with everything. Matthew was much calmer throughout this entire process than I was, or at least he appeared calm. He was amazing during labor and even when we brought the babies home and they were crying, he tried to soothe them the best he could. His mother let us know it could be the change of environment for them. Once they are adjusted, they may stop crying so much.

On the bright side of things, it felt so much better to have them home. I could look at their beautiful faces all day, and that for sure helped ease my mind. Matthew made me laugh because he would confuse the twins and mistake them for each other. While they were in the hospital, we ordered name bracelets for them, but they hadn't arrived yet. Those would come in handy for him and anyone else that got confused. They were mine, so I knew who was who.

Later that day, some of Matthew and I's friends came over to see the babies. So that meant I had to get dressed and look presentable. That was going to be a task for the both of us. We were extremely tired, but I didn't want to tell them no. Everyone was just as excited as we were about the babies. But I felt like we'd had our fair share of visitors for a while. After today I planned to tell Matthew we needed a visitation break. It was nice to see everyone, and I was so thankful they wanted to stop by. But I wanted to make sure we were getting enough rest during the twin's nap times. That day, some of the saints stopped by and it was so nice to see their faces. Especially since I hadn't been to church in about three weeks, since before the birth and probably wouldn't anytime soon. At least for another few weeks or so until we figured out how to manage both of them without getting too fussy. I was sure that Matthew would return before I did. They were all so excited for us and told us how beautiful the babies were.

Mother Massy, who was by far one of my favorites, came to visit as well. She was so proud of me and Matthew. Especially Matthew since she'd been with him since he started the church; they had a special bond. She stayed the longest, which I didn't mind and came bearing gifts, as everyone did. We already had so much stuff from our baby shower. And everyone that came to visit brought even more stuff for us, food, clothes, and more food; It felt so good to be loved. Mother Massy ended up being the last one to come. She stayed with us for dinner, as we ate some of the food the other members and friends brought before she headed home. I took a short bath and laid down with my babies. They had a really good feed before they fell asleep. I hoped that meant they would sleep a little better tonight.

—

Looking at my wife and daughters brings me so much joy. I am still in awe of everything that has transpired. Mariah was amazing during labor and pushed both the babies out with ease. When I first held them, I was stunned. They were beautiful and their cries were music to my ears. As soon as the doctor placed the first baby on Mariah's stomach, she immediately started crying. Seeing how happy she was turned out to be a much more fulfilling moment than I thought. I couldn't help but to cry myself. When they told us, they had to keep the babies in the NICU, I wasn't surprised, but I was sad, as they warned us this could happen. I didn't worry though, instead I prayed they would be okay. I remember the worry on Mariah's face, but I reminded her who has the final say in everything and that they would be okay. Less than a week later, we were able to bring them home and reality set in quickly. They cried the first night, keeping Mariah and her mom up most the night. Once they went to sleep, Mariah was able to get some rest and I took them when they woke up the second time. We've introduced the bottle to them, but I think they may like breastfeeding more. My poor wife would be worn out. I promised I'd do everything I could to help her. After all the visitors today, I figured she would be tired. I hope they sleep a little better for her tonight. I sure could use the rest as well. I am so thankful for everything that has transpired so far. Mariah has been an amazing wife and first lady and I know she will be an amazing mother. I am so excited to see what the future holds for us.

Chapter 28:

Dreams Do Come True

Wow! It's been over a year and I can't believe where I am now. My babies are now one and walking all around the house! We've had to childproof everything like the doors, locks, and outlets. They are even starting to talk and say short sentences and words. So far, they've said mama, dada, sister and different types of food. They are growing up right before my eyes and I'm not sure how to feel about it. I want them to stay babies forever, but I know that isn't realistic. They've both come such a long way since their entrance into the world. The doctors kept telling us to watch for different signs because it could be an indication for a problem. But, they showed no negative signs and kept exceeding the learning marks for their ages. The doctors can make you feel worried and unsure because they're always preparing for the worse to happen. Matthew was great at making sure we kept everything in perspective and to celebrate every milestone they accomplished. As soon as we went back to church, we dedicated them to God and that meant we had nothing to worry about. It seemed like just two months ago Mathew and I met. Days later we got married and then yesterday my water broke, and I was in the hospital experiencing harsh labor pains. Everything went so fast.

I am still happy as I can be working at the firm and for the DA's office. Being a lawyer never seems to faze me. There is always someone who thinks they can commit a murder, leave every traceable clue behind and assume they won't get caught. That's where the DA and I come in. We put those criminals behind bars for good. Working with the DA's office has its perks, as I sometimes get to view cases before they're officially sent out. I can often contact some of the victims, introduce myself, and let them know I'd be willing to represent them. That can often take the weight and stress off finding a lawyer. Especially when something traumatic has just happened. At the firm, I've been working on corporate and business cases which I also enjoy. Those usually end up being mediation cases and often quicker than criminal cases. I like that I have a variety of things to do within my day.

Matthew is an extreme math nerd. He loves numbers and loves helping others with their finances. He recently started training future graduate students in his line of work to be accountants and financial advisors. Training the college students really makes him happy. He always says how most of them are so eager to learn and work. He's also excited that he not only gets to share his knowledge of accounting with others, but he gets to "talk numbers with someone who understands", as he says. I must admit, that is something we don't have in common. I rarely understand what he's talking about, but I sit and listen anyway. Some of the students he gets are just there to meet the program requirements, which for him, takes the fun away. But overall, he still enjoys it.

The church is doing so well, and no one is stealing from the offering anymore. After Matthew changed the way offering was done, it seemed to go back to some normalcy. Deacon Patterson never admitted to stealing any money, but it was kind of evident that he was. His demeanor changed for a while and he and his wife stopped coming to church. After about 2 months, they came back and assumed their regular duties. Matthew welcomed them back with open arms and we continued church as normal. We've also gained a few new members. A few couples had babies and a family joined the church that just moved from Florida. The church is growing, and Matthew is excited. I think I'm beginning to get the hang of being a first lady and all that it has to offer. And I also got used to the name. I often found my faith being tested, as people came to me looking for answers and encouragement. After the babies came, I was in a bit of a slump adjusting to everything. I realized I was dealing with a little postpartum depression, on top of all the recent life changes I was experiencing. But that didn't stop people from wanting prayer, and I found strength I didn't know I had. I wondered how Matthew always did it so graciously. He always reminded me I was made for this.

Our parents still come and visit us every so often, as their help is always needed. Matthew and I decided to hire a nanny because between my job and his job, it was impossible to manage all of that. I didn't feel comfortable taking them to daycare, so we hired someone we were both familiar with.

I can honestly say I've grown so much within the last year. Matthew continues to prove to me he's the best husband ever. No matter what mood I'm in, he always knows what to say to cheer me up. He was so supportive after the twins came while I was trying to find my way. I quickly realized I wasn't the only one adjusting in the relationship, which made me sensitive to his needs as well. My love for him continues to develop into something new every day. God really did a work when he made Matthew and allowed our paths to cross; it's like we were made for each other. Our relationship continues to grow as we learn more about each other and how to be better parents. We even started discussing the possibility of trying for a boy. I wasn't sure how I'd feel about having more children after the twins, but all the pain was definitely worth it. And it would be wonderful if I could give Matthew a son.

Life in LA is amazing! I love the weather, the people, and all that LA has brought me. It took a little time to get used to and find my own way, but I did it. I'm much closer to my sister now, which is a bonus for both of us. We don't have any other family in California but each other, so it was important that we kept in touch. We've fallen off our weekly dates, it's more like monthly now but we still see each other often. She's a great auntie and the girls really love her. I've met an amazing friend here as well as my fantastic paralegal. Together, we have kicked some major law butt. Looking back over the past three years, I would never have seen myself in this spot and I know I only have room to grow. As long as I put God first in whatever I do, I know that good will come to me.

To sum everything up, God gave me More Than I ever wanted.

About the author:

Deszane' Flowers was born and raised in Denver, Colorado. Deszane' considers her faith and family to be the most important aspects in her life, which she hoped to portray in this novel. She has always had a passion for writing and hopes to inspire others to reach their full potential and to use all the gifts God has given them. More than I Ever Wanted is Deszanes' first book, with hopes of many more to come.